house of
dark
shadows

BOOKS BY THIS AUTHOR

Comes a Horseman

Germ

Deadfall

DREAMHOUSE KINGS SERIES

1 House of Dark Shadows

2 Watcher in the Woods

house of dark shadows

BOOK ONE OF
DREAMHOUSE KINGS

ROBERT LIPARULO

THOMAS NELSON
Since 1798

NASHVILLE DALLAS MEXICO CITY RIO DE JANEIRO BEIJING

Published in Nashville, Tennessee, by Thomas Nelson. Thomas Nelson is a registered trademark of Thomas Nelson, Inc.

Page design by Mandi Cofer
Map design by Doug Cordes

Thomas Nelson, Inc., titles may be purchased in bulk for educational, business, fund-raising, or sales promotional use. For information, please e-mail SpecialMarkets@ThomasNelson.com.

ISBN 978-1-59554-563-3 (trade paper SE)

Library of Congress Cataloging-in-Publication Data

Liparulo, Robert.
    House of dark shadows / Robert Liparulo.
        p. cm. — (Dream house Kings ; bk. 1)
        Summary: When fifteen-year-old Xander and his family move into an old, abandoned house in the middle of a dense forest outside of a small California town, they discover that not only are some of the rooms portals into other places, but that malevolent forces are at work.
        ISBN 978-1-59554-494-0 (hardcover)
        [1. Supernatural—Fiction. 2. Dwellings—Fiction. 3. Family life—California—Fiction. 4. California—Fiction. 5. Horror stories.]
        I. Title.
        PZ7.L6636Ho 2008
        [Fic]—dc22

        2008004620

Printed in the United States of America
08 09 10 11 RRD 6 5 4 3 2 1

TO MY SON ANTHONY,

whose enthusiastic and energetic spirit
makes our home as adventurous as
(but eternally brighter than)
the house in this story.

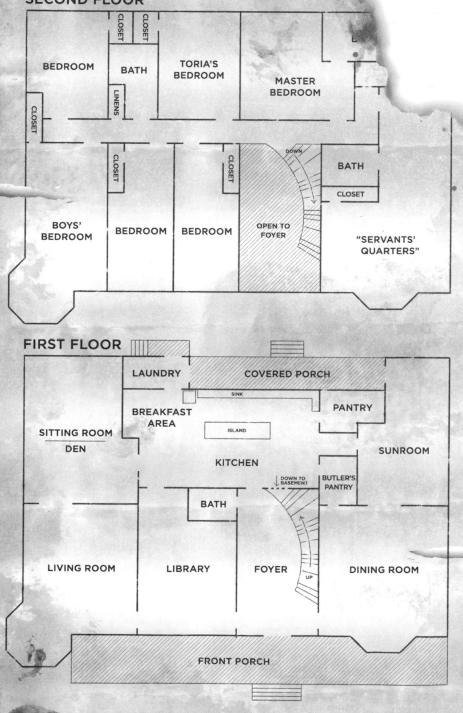

SECOND FLOOR

BEDROOM

CLOSET

CLOSET

BATH

LINENS

TORIA'S BEDROOM

MASTER BEDROOM

CLOSET

DOWN

BATH

CLOSET

BOYS' BEDROOM

CLOSET

BEDROOM

BEDROOM

CLOSET

OPEN TO FOYER

"SERVANTS' QUARTERS"

FIRST FLOOR

LAUNDRY

COVERED PORCH

SINK

BREAKFAST AREA

PANTRY

SITTING ROOM

DEN

ISLAND

KITCHEN

SUNROOM

DOWN TO BASEMENT

BUTLER'S PANTRY

BATH

LIVING ROOM

LIBRARY

FOYER

UP

DINING ROOM

FRONT PORCH

"A house of which one knows every room isn't worth living in."

—GIUSEPPE TOMASI DI LAMPEDUSA

PROLOGUE

THIRTY YEARS AGO

The walls of the house absorbed the woman's screams, until they felt to her as muffled and pointless as yelling underwater. Still, her lungs kept pushing out cries for help. Her attacker carried her over his shoulder. The stench of his sweat filled her nostrils. He paid no heed to her frantic writhing, or the pounding of her fists on his back, or even her fingernails, which dug furrows into his flesh. He simply lumbered, as steadily as a freight train, through the corridors of the big house.

She knew where they were heading but not where she would end up. In this house nothing was normal, nothing as it appeared. So while she knew in advance the turns her attacker would take, which hallways and doors he would traverse, their destination was as unknowable as a faraway galaxy. And that meant her *taking* would be untraceable. She would be unreachable to searchers. To would-be rescuers. To her *family*—and that realization terrified her more than being grabbed out of her bed. More than the flashes of imagined cruelty she would suffer away from the protection of the people who loved her. More than death.

But then she saw something more terrifying: her children, scrambling to catch up, to help. Their eyes were wide, streaming. They stumbled up the narrow staircase behind her attacker, seeming far below, rising to meet her. The thought of them following her into the chasm of her fate was more than she could stand.

"Go back," she said, but by this time her throat was raw, her voice weak.

The man reached the landing and turned into another corridor.

Temporarily out of sight, her son yelled, "Mom!" His seven-year-old voice was almost lost in the shrillness of his panic. He appeared on the landing. His socked feet slipped on the hardwood floor, and he went down. Behind him, his little sister stopped. She was frightened and confused, too young to do anything more than follow her brother. He clambered up and started to run again.

A hand gripped his shoulder, jarring him back.

The boy's father had something in his fist: the lamp from his nightstand! He passed the boy in the hallway. His bare feet gave him traction.

Thank God, she thought.

He reached her in seconds. With the lamp raised over his head, he grabbed her wrist. He pulled, tried to anchor himself to the floor, to the carpeted runner now covering the wood planks. But the brute under her walked on, tugging him with them. The man yanked on her arm. Pain flared in her shoulder. He might as well have tried pulling her from a car as it sped past.

She caught a glimpse of the bizarrely shaped light fixtures on the corridor walls—mostly carved faces with glowing eyes. The bulbs flickered in time with her racing heart. She could not remember any of the lights doing that before. It was as though the electrical current running through the wires was responding to a disruption in the way things were *supposed* to be, a glitch in reality.

"Henry," she said, pleading, hopeful.

His grip tightened as he stumbled along behind them. He brought the lamp's heavy base down on her assailant. If the man carrying her flinched, she did not feel it. If he grunted or yelled out, she did not hear it.

What he did was stop. He spun around so quickly, the woman's husband lost his grip on her. And now facing the other direction, she lost sight of him. Being suddenly denied her husband's visage felt like getting the wind knocked out of her. She realized he was face-to-face with the man who'd taken her, and *that* felt like watching him step off a cliff.

"Nooo!" she screamed, her voice finding some volume. "Henry!"

His hand gripped her ankle, then broke free. The man under her moved in a violent dance, jostling her wildly. He spun again and her head struck the wall.

The lights went out completely . . . but no, not the lights . . . her consciousness. It came back to her slowly, like the warmth of fire on a blustery day.

She tasted blood. She'd bitten her tongue. She opened her eyes. Henry was crumpled on the floor, receding as she was carried away. The children stood over him, touching him, calling him. Her son's eyes found hers again. Determination hardened his jaw, pushed away the fear . . . at least a measure of it. He stepped over his father's legs, coming to her rescue. Henry raised his head, weary, stunned. He reached for the boy, but missed.

Over the huffing breath of the man, the soft patter of her son's feet reached her ears. How she'd loved that sound, knowing it was bringing him to her. Now she wanted it to carry him away away from this danger. Her husband called to him in a croaking, strained voice. The boy kept coming.

She spread her arms. Her left hand clutched at open air, but the right one touched a wall. She clawed at it. Her nails snagged the wallpaper. One nail peeled back from her finger and snapped off.

Her assailant turned again, into a room—one of the small antechambers, like a mud room before the *real* room. He strode straight toward the next threshold.

Her son reached the first door, catching it as it was closing.

"Mom!" Panic etched old-man lines into his young face. His eyes appeared as wide as his mouth. He banged his shoulder on the jamb, trying to hurry in.

"Stay!" she said. She showed him her palms in a "stop" gesture, hoping he would understand, hoping he would obey. She took in his face, as a diver takes in a deep breath before plunging into the depths. He was fully in the antechamber now, reaching for her with both arms, but her captor had already opened the second door and was stepping through. The door was swinging shut behind him.

The light they were stepping into was bright. It swept around her, through the opening, and made pinpoints of the boy's irises. His blue eyes dazzled. His cheeks glistened with tears. He wore his favorite pajamas—little R2-D2s and C-3POs all over them, threadbare and too small for him.

"I—" she started, meaning to say she loved him, but the brute bounded downward, driving his shoulder into her stomach.

Air rushed from her, unformed by vocal cords, tongue, lips. Just air.

"Moooom!" her son screamed. Full of despair. Reaching. Almost to the door. "Mo—"

The door closed, separating her from her family forever.

one

"Nothing but trees," the bear said in Xander's voice. It repeated itself: "Nothing but trees."

Xander King turned away from the car window and stared into the smiling furry face, with its shiny half-bead eyes and stitched-on nose. "I mean it, Toria," he said. "Get that thing out of my face. And turn it off."

His sister's hands moved quickly over the teddy bear's paws, all the while keeping it suspended three inches in front of Xander. The bear repeated, "I mean it, Toria. Get that—"

At fifteen years old, Xander was too old to be messing around with little-kid toys. He seized the bear, squeezing the paw that silenced it.

"Mom!" Toria yelled. "Make him give Wuzzy back!" She grabbed for it.

Xander turned away from her, tucking Wuzzy between his body and the car door. Outside his window, nothing but trees—as he had said and Wuzzy had echoed. It reminded him of a movie, as almost everything did. This time it was *The Edge*, about a bear intent on eating Anthony Hopkins. An opening shot of the wilderness where it was filmed showed miles and miles of lush forest. *Nothing but trees.*

A month ago his dad had announced that he had accepted a position as principal of a school six hundred miles away, and the whole King family had to move from the only home Xander had ever known. They were going to a place he had never even heard of: Pinedale, almost straight north from their home in Pasadena. Still in California, but barely. Pinedale. The name itself said "hick," "small," and "If you don't die here, you'll wish you had." Of course, he had screamed, begged, sulked, and threatened to run away. But in the end here he was, wedged in the back seat with his nine-year-old sister and twelve-year-old brother.

The longer they drove, the thicker the woods grew, and

the more miserable he became. It was bad enough leaving his friends, his school—*everything!*—but to be leaving them for Hicksville, in the middle of nowhere, was a stake through his heart.

"Mom!" Toria yelled again, reaching for the bear.

Xander squeezed closer to the door, away from her. He must have put pressure on the bear in the wrong place: it began chanting in Toria's whiny voice: "Mom! Mom! Mom!"

He frantically squeezed Wuzzy's paws, but could not make it stop.

"Mom! Mom! Mom!"

The controls in the bear's arms weren't working. Frustrated by its continuous one-word poking at his brain—and a little concerned he had broken it and would have to buy her a new one—he looked to his sister for help.

She wasn't grabbing for it anymore. Just grinning. One of those see-what-happens-when-you-mess-with-me smiles.

"Mom! Mom! Mom!"

Xander was about to show her what happened when you messed with *him*—the possibilities ranged from a display of his superior vocal volume to ripping Wuzzy's arms right off—when the absurdity of it struck him. He cracked up.

"I mean it," he laughed. "This thing is driving me crazy." He shook the bear at her. It continued yelling for their mother.

His brother, David, who was sitting on the other side of Toria and who had been doing a good job of staying out of the fight, started laughing too. He mimicked the bear, who was mimicking their sister: "Mom! Mom! Mom!"

Mrs. King shifted around in the front passenger seat. She was smiling, but her eyes were curious.

"Xander broke Wuzzy!" Toria whined. "He won't turn off." She pulled the bear out of Xander's hands.

The furry beast stopped talking: "Mo—" Then, blessed silence.

Toria looked from brother to brother, and they laughed again.

Xander shrugged. "I guess he just doesn't like me."

"He only likes *me*," Toria said, hugging it.

"Oh brother," David said. He went back to the PSP game that had kept him occupied most of the drive.

Mom raised her eyebrows at Xander and said, "Be nice."

Xander rolled his eyes. He adjusted his shoulders and wiggled his behind, nudging Toria. "It's too cramped back here. It may be an SUV, but it isn't big enough for us anymore."

"Don't start that," his father warned from behind the wheel. He angled the rearview mirror to see his son.

"What?" Xander said, acting innocent.

"I did the same thing with my father," Dad said. "The car's too small . . . it uses too much gas . . . it's too run down . . ."

Xander smiled. "Well, it is."

"And if we get a new car, what should we do with this one?"

"Well . . ." Xander said. "You know. It'd be a safe car for me." A ten-year-old Toyota 4Runner wasn't his idea of cool wheels, but it *was* transportation.

Dad nodded. "Getting you a car is something we can talk about, okay? Let's see how you do."

"I have my driver's permit. You *know* I'm a good driver."

"He is," Toria chimed in.

David added, "And then he can drive us to school."

"I didn't mean just the driving," Dad said. He paused, catching Xander's eyes in the mirror. "I mean with all of this, the move and everything."

Xander stared out the window again. He mumbled, "Guess I'll never get a car, then."

"Xander?" Dad said. "I didn't hear that."

"Nothing."

"He said he'll never get a car," Toria said.

Silence. David's thumbs clicked furiously over the PSP buttons. Xander was aware of his mom watching him. If he looked, her eyes would be all sad-like, and she would be frowning in sympathy for him. He thought maybe his dad was looking too, but only for an opportunity to explain himself again. Xander didn't want to hear it. Nothing his old man said would make this okay, would make ripping him out of his world less awful than it was.

"Dad, is the school's soccer team good? Did they place?" David asked. Xander knew his brother wasn't happy about the move either, but jumping right into the sport he was so obsessed about went a long way toward making the change something he could handle. Maybe Xander was like that three years ago, just rolling with the punches. He couldn't remember. But now he had things in his life David didn't: friends who truly mattered, ones he thought he'd spend the rest of his life with. Little kids didn't think that way. Friends could come and go, and they adjusted. True, Xander had known his current friends for years, but they hadn't become like *blood* until the last year or so.

That got him thinking about Danielle. He pulled his mobile phone from his shirt pocket and checked it. No text messages from her. No calls. She hadn't replied to the last text he'd sent. He keyed in another: "Forget me already? JK." But he wasn't Just Kidding. He knew the score: out of sight, out of mind. She had said all the right things, like *We'll talk on the phone all the time; You come down and see me and I'll come up to see you, okay?* and *I'll wait for you.*

Yeah, sure you will, he thought. Even during the past week, he'd sensed a coldness in her, an emotional distancing. When he'd told his best friend, Dean had shrugged. Trying to sound world-wise, he'd said, "Forget her, dude. She's hot. She's gotta move on. You too. Not like you're married, right?" Dean had never liked Danielle.

Xander tried to convince himself she was just another friend he was forced to leave behind. But there was a different kind of ache in his chest when he thought about her. A heavy weight in his stomach.

Stop it! he told himself. He flipped his phone closed.

On his mental list of the reasons to hate the move to Pinedale, he moved on to the one titled "career." He had just started making short films with his buddies and was pretty sure it was something he would eventually do for a living. They weren't much, just short skits he and his friends acted out. He and Dean wrote the scripts, did the filming, used computer software to edit an hour of video into five-minute films, and laid music over them. They had six already on YouTube—with an average rating of four and a half stars and a boatload of praise. Xander had dreams of getting a short film into the festival circuit, which, of course, would lead to offers to do music videos and commercials, then on to feature movies starring the next Russell Crowe and Jim Carrey, and probably an Oscar. Pasadena was right next to Hollywood, a twenty-minute drive. You couldn't ask for a better place to live if you were the next Steven Spielberg. What on earth would he find to film in Pinedale? *Trees,* he thought glumly, watching them fly past his window.

Dad, addressing David's soccer concern, said, "We'll talk about it later."

Mom reached through the seat backs to shake Xander's knee. "It'll work out," she whispered.

"Wait a minute," David said, understanding Dad-talk as well

as Xander did. "Are you saying they suck—or that they don't *have* a soccer team? You told me they did!"

"I said 'later,' Dae." His nickname came from Toria's inability as a toddler to say David. She had also called Xander *Xan*, but it hadn't stuck.

David slumped down in his seat.

Xander let the full extent of his misery show on his face for his mother.

She gave his knee a shake, sharing his misery. She was good that way. "Give it some time," she whispered. "You'll make new friends and find new things to do. Wait and see."

CHAPTER

two

Their motel room was decorated like a six-year-old boy's bedroom. Athletes doing their thing illustrated the wallpaper, bedspreads, hand towels, shower curtain. The bedside lamp was a cartoon-faced baseball player, whose bat held up the bulb and shade. A throw rug between the beds was supposed to look like a giant basketball, but time and lots of feet had worn it into something more like a squashed pumpkin.

"Who do they think stays here?" Xander said, noticing someone had painted red stitching on the globe of the ceiling light in an effort to make it resemble a baseball. When he pointed it out to David, his brother thought it was supposed to be a bloodshot eye. They were sitting on the bed that, unbelievably, they would have to share until his parents arranged for something more permanent. Xander was going to make darned sure no one fed the kid beans before then.

"The décor is . . . *interesting,*" Mrs. King said. Usually she found something charming or at least educational about everything. That she didn't this time validated Xander's suspicion that the motel owners were totally clueless.

"I like the soccer players," David said.

"No, really?" Xander pushed him hard enough to send him flying off the bed and onto the road-kill pumpkin.

One thing Xander appreciated about David was his determination to stand up for himself. Instead of crying for Mommy every time Xander did something he didn't like, he either turned a cold shoulder or fought back. This time he fought back. Smiling, he sprung off the floor and tackled Xander back onto the bed.

Xander rolled, so he was sitting on his brother. He grabbed David's wrists and tried to pin him. David jerked his arms free and landed a blow to Xander's stomach. Xander jabbed David in the ribs and got a solid grip on his wrists. He pinned his hands to the bed, one next to each of David's ears. He made a noise in his throat that implied the gathering of something worth spitting onto his brother's face. David began to squirm, tighten his face, and thrash his head from side to side.

"Boys!" Mom said.

"Ah, let 'em be," Dad told her. "They just spent nine hours in the car."

David heaved his legs up behind Xander and drove a knee into his back.

"Ahh!" Xander yelled.

David pulled an arm free, reached up, and grabbed a handful of Xander's hair.

Xander squeezed his eyes shut. "David . . . let go!"

"Get off me."

"*Let go.*"

Somewhere in the room, Mom pleaded to Dad. "Ed?"

"G, they're fine."

It hadn't been until Xander was in kindergarten, when the other kids had laughed, that he realized G—as in "gee whiz"— was a funny name for a mom . . . for anybody. His mother had explained that she simply did not feel like a Gertrude, and even at that young age, Xander had agreed that G was much better. In fact, the family had developed a saying whenever Mom did something bold or crazy—like getting in the face of the line-backer-sized neighbor who'd yelled at David to get off his yard or parasailing behind a speedboat in Baja: *definitely not a Gertrude.*

"Okay, okay," Xander said. Slowly, he slid off his brother.

David held on until Xander had shifted his entire weight from David's belly to the bed. David pulled his knees up to his chest, preventing Xander from jumping on again. Then he cautiously released his grip on Xander's hair. Before David could spin away, Xander spat, nailing his brother's cheek. Xander howled in laughter and bolted for the door. He yanked it open and darted into the parking lot.

"Alexander!" his mother yelled after him. "You get back here right now!"

But Dad called to them, "Not too far, guys!" giving him permission to continue on.

The door slammed. Heading for a big field beyond the parking lot, Xander looked back to see David sprinting after him. He was still wiping his face.

CHAPTER

three

The man in the house lumbered through the corridor. He could tell right away nothing had changed. It was the same dark, empty place it had been time after time. But it was his duty to check. So with a deep sigh, he moved through a threshold into the next room. His shoulders scraped both sides of the door frame. The weight of each footstep rattled the windows and caused the floor to groan under him. His eyes were accustomed to darkness, but still he squinted at the shadows gathered in each room. He grunted at them, and when he was satisfied they were only shadows after all, he moved on.

A spider dropped from the ceiling, landing on his shoulder. He swiped at it, smearing the grime and sweat already there. It darted to his chest, where he flattened it with a palm the size of a Ping-Pong paddle. Having made his usual circuit through hallways, stairways, and rooms, he heaved his heavy shoulders in a deep, sad breath and headed for the door that would take him home.

Something stopped him. A sound. He turned and retraced his steps to the front rooms. He looked out a leaded glass window. Through a patina of filth, he saw a man approaching. He was ambling through the trees slowly, cautiously. He did not move directly to the door, but cut diagonally to the side of the house.

The man inside moved with him, from window to window. The outsider returned to the front. He went toward the door but did not come close. He seemed satisfied and began walking away, his gait more confident. At the window, the man inside shifted his considerable weight from one foot to the other. A floorboard creaked.

The other man stopped to look. He appeared to stare directly at the man inside. But it was dark in the house, and if the other saw him, he gave no clue. He walked on, glancing back only once more.

For a while, the man watched his breath condense and evaporate on the window. Then he turned and went home.

CHAPTER

four

SATURDAY, 6:58 P.M.

Halfway through the field, almost back to the hotel, Xander reached out and brushed the most obvious grass out of his brother's hair.

David smiled. "Thanks."

Xander shrugged. "Don't want to get in trouble for pounding on you."

David appraised him. "Who pounded on who?"

Xander pushed him. "Look at you."

"*You're* the one limping."

"Yeah, right," Xander said, trying to ignore the pain in his ankle.

"If the cops stop us, I'll tell them you're a mugger."

"I don't think they have muggers here," Xander said. "Besides, they'd have to be blind to not know we're brothers." They both had dark brown hair, though Xander's was longer and shaggier. Same smile. And while David had their mother's hazel eyes and Xander his dad's blue, they shared an eye shape that was sort of like a teardrop lying on its side. There were times when each of them had mistaken David for Xander and vice-versa in photographs. Even Dad had done that, but never Mom; she always knew, and without squinting at them to be sure, the way Dad did.

"It's going to be cool," David said, "us being in the same school again, huh?"

"Maybe." Pinedale was so small, it had only one elementary school and another school that served seventh through twelfth grades. It had been five years since the brothers attended the same school at the same time, when David was in second grade and Xander fifth.

"Are we going to find a house before school starts, you think?"

"That's the plan, but it's a lot to do in a week."

"Car's gone," David announced.

Xander looked up to see that the 4Runner was not in the motel parking lot. He said, "Dad probably went out for food."

"Good. I'm starving."

When they entered, Toria and Mom were sitting on Toria's rollaway bed. They were looking at brochures for what the locals thought were visitor attractions. Toria had picked them up at a gas station outside of town. She was always looking for something to read, was almost never without a book or newspaper. She even read the sports section, for crying out loud.

"Dad went for some grub," Mom said.

"When'll he be back? I could eat a whole cow," David said.

"Gross," Toria said.

Mom checked the bedside clock. "Should have been back by now. Probably making new friends. You know your father."

"McD's?" he asked hopefully.

She smiled. "'Fraid you're heading for a junk food withdrawal, Dae. None of that here. There's a café up the street. Bet you like it."

David looked at Xander, neither of them so sure.

"Did you know this is the capital of Bigfoot country?" Toria asked.

Xander made a face. "Bigfoot?"

"Yeah," she said, consulting the brochure in her hands. "There have been more sightings in this area than anywhere else in the United States. People have launched expeditions to find him, right from Pinedale."

"So?" Xander said. "Did they find him?"

"If they did," she said, "it would've been in the news. But there's a Bigfoot museum in town."

23

The door opened and Dad stepped in, a brown grocery bag in one arm. The smell of roasted chicken filled the room. "Dinner's on," he announced.

David said, "Oh yeah!"

They sat at a table near the door. It was chipped Formica with what looked like stickers of sporting equipment plastered all over it.

As she heaped meat and potato salad onto paper plates, Mom said, "Eat up! I want us to get to bed early. We have a busy day tomorrow."

"Doing what?" Xander asked.

"House hunting."

Xander made a face. "All of us?"

"Would you rather stay here and babysit?"

"No, thanks."

"I thought we could swing by and see your new schools too."

"Noooo," David moaned.

"Oh, come on!" Xander said. "We're in town less than twenty-four hours and we have to go see the *school*?"

Mom said, "You want to see it before your first day, don't you?"

"I can wait," Xander said.

"It won't be so bad. You'll see," Dad said, shaking a forkful of chicken at him. "Now eat."

CHAPTER

five

The next morning, during breakfast at the same café where Dad had bought their chicken dinner, Mom wondered about the local churches.

Dad frowed and looked at his watch. "I haven't had a chance . . ."

Mom shook her head. "Mr. King, next week for sure. No excuses."

Dad smiled. "Absolutely."

Twenty minutes later, the Kings found themselves in front of Pinedale Middle and Senior High School. Xander could not find the right words to describe it. Okay, it had a nice setting—quaint, peaceful. Situated up a forested hill, it overlooked the town. On three sides the tree-covered hills continued, giving the school a lush, green backdrop. The building itself was a brick single-story. L-shaped. In the square yard between the wings were grass, several flat-rock patios, picnic tables, and a flagpole. *A lot like a park*, he thought. Still, it was a *school*.

"Pretty, isn't it?" his mother said.

"It's okay," he answered, shrugging. "Does *pretty* really matter when it comes to education?" Trying to sound enlightened.

She gave him a dirty look. "Hey, you're the one who has to look at it for the next three years, not me."

They all climbed out of the SUV. From their vantage point in the front parking lot, marked VISITORS AND FACULTY ONLY, they could see the end zone and scoreboard of a football field around back.

David pointed to the statue of an animal leaping over the scoreboard. "Their mascot's a cougar. That's cool."

"Panther," Dad said. "Pinedale Panthers."

"That's cool too."

Mom crossed the pickup lane and stepped into the grassy area. "Come on, let's have a look."

David, forgetting himself, ran to catch up. Toria followed.

Dad stepped up next to Xander. He patted his son on the back, then laid his hand on Xander's shoulder. He said, "Not interested?"

"I'll see enough of it after next week."

"I know it's tough to change schools. I did a lot of that."

Xander turned to him. "So that makes it okay?"

"I'm not saying that. Just . . ." Dad seemed to search for the right words. "I wouldn't have done this to you if it wasn't important."

"Important to who?"

"Us. The family. Me."

"That's the part I don't get. Why is it important? I thought you liked being a teacher. I thought you liked Valley High."

"I did. I—" Dad looked up at the sky. After a few moments, he lowered his eyes to Xander's. "You gotta trust me on this, okay?"

Xander turned away, pretending to watch Mom, Dae, and Toria scope out the school. *Did* he have to trust him? It wasn't really *trusting* him he had to do, was it? It was really about going along with his plan, because he was a kid and couldn't do anything else. Not yet.

He said, "Sounds like you don't have a good reason."

"I do," his father said. "I just can't . . . I can't get into it right now with you. When I can I will."

Xander bowed his head. *What is this?* he thought. Dad had a secret reason for moving all of them to Pinedale? Or was it Pasadena he was moving them *from?* Was he going *to* something or running *from* something? A hundred possibilities occurred to him at once: Was his father in the Witness Protection Program? Had he discovered a treasure map and was determined to make them all rich? Had he had an affair, and distancing all of them from the other woman was the only way to hold the family together? Nothing sounded right. But it had to be *something*. Probably it was a midlife crisis or something else equally lame.

"Son," his father continued, "don't think you're here simply because I want to be and I have to bring you along. You're not baggage or furniture. I *need* you."

"But you can't tell me why." Xander held his lips tight.

His father's shoulders slumped. He looked miserable. He said, "Not yet."

"When?"

"Soon, I promise. But don't fight me on this, as hard as it is for you . . . please." He extended his hand to Xander, wanting to seal his son's compliance with a shake.

Xander knew his dad was trying to bridge a gap. He stared at the hand, then grabbed it. He let a weak smile bend his lips.

He said, "I'll try to do better."

"That's all I'm asking for." Dad cocked his head at the school. "Wanna check it out?"

They started walking. Dad kept his palm pressed to Xander's back. Mom, David, and Toria were gazing into different windows.

"Classroom," Mom called out.

"Here's the library," David informed her.

Toria said something Xander couldn't make out.

Dad and Xander stepped onto the open area's grass. It was thick and impossibly green. It felt like an exercise mat under Xander's feet.

"I still want to go home," he said.

"I know, Son." He slid his hand to Xander's shoulder, squeezed it. "I know."

A few paces farther, Xander said, "Dad?"

"Hmm?"

"If I guess your secret, will you tell me if I'm right?"

His father laughed but didn't answer.

CHAPTER

Six

Two hours later, they had seen three properties that were for sale.

It was clear to Xander his parents were looking for something completely different from the suburban house they had left. The lots were large and thick with trees, the houses more like the hunting cabins he had seen in movies—cabins where college kids seek shelter from ax-wielding madmen or ticked-off ghosts. In those movies, the cabins were never shelter enough.

One house he and David liked was situated down a slope from the road, nearly invisible through the trees. A river—Dad said it was Weaver Creek—cut so close to the house, Xander thought they could fish from the back deck. The water rushed over boulders, making a surflike sound. All Mom could see was a deathtrap and refused to discuss the possibility of buying it.

Xander didn't mind the secluded settings. He figured that since there wasn't a multiplex or mall within two hundred miles, and given the choice of forested isolation or depressing little cafés and retail shops, he'd rather live near Mother Nature. He started to view the properties from an outdoorsman's perspective: hiking alone in the woods; dirt biking over the rugged terrain; campfires and pup tents within sight of a refrigerator and bathroom.

Each property took them farther from the school but never so far that he couldn't bike it when he had to. If he got a car, he wouldn't care if they found a place in the next county. In fact, he was starting to get into the tight, winding roads that snaked away from Pinedale in four directions. He could easily see himself behind the wheel of a '68 Corvette convertible—327-cubic-inch engine, tuned exhaust, four-on-the-floor—nudging the speedometer on each turn until the tires squealed in fear.

Dad consulted a stack of property listings, which he had printed from a local Realtor's Web site. He put the car in gear and backed out of the gravel driveway.

Mom turned in the seat. "So what do you think so far?"

"I liked the one with the river," David said quickly.

"Will I get my own room?" Toria asked.

"*You* will," Mom said, and the way she said it made Xander ask, "What about us?" He and David had shared a bedroom for twelve years, and he'd thought if anything good came out of the move, it might be finally getting his own room.

"It depends," she said. "These houses really aren't that big."

"I noticed, but there's lots of land. Could we add on?"

"Hey!" David said, clearly liking the idea.

"Whoa," Dad said, "additions are expensive."

Xander rolled his eyes. *Everything* was expensive. When Dad started talking costs, it meant it wasn't going to happen.

Dad switched on the blinker to turn left, waited for an oncoming car to pass, then pulled the 4Runner onto a narrow, paved road. The forest here was especially dense. They crowded the road and in spots formed leafy tunnels through which Dad drove.

"What if we do it ourselves?" David asked.

Dad glanced back. "Do what?"

"Build our own bedrooms." His big grin told Xander he had all sorts of ideas for a room. Xander shook his head at David and mouthed the words *no way.*

"I don't think so," Dad said. After a moment, he said, "You know, *maybe.*" He smiled back at David. "That's not such a bad idea."

David made wide eyes at Xander, whose face was slack in

disbelief. Dad hadn't even said he'd think about it. "Not such a bad idea" in Dad-talk was *yes.*

The 4Runner pulled onto a dirt road. While David rambled on about skylights and secret rooms behind hidden panels, Xander studied the forest on his side of the car. Foliage and shadows limited visibility to twenty or thirty feet from the edge of the road. He would be the first to admit that he knew as much about trees and the woods as he did about Thailand, but he couldn't help but think that there was something different about *this* forest. The leaves of different trees seemed to sway in opposing directions, more like they were controlled by the trees themselves than by the wind. Shadows shifted oddly. The darkness rushed at the car, stopping just feet from the forest's edge, then it pulled way back, exposing gnarled trunks and spindly branches deep within the forest. It reminded him of the surf, flowing in and out, but much quicker and without a discernible pattern. He knew the swaying leaves and branches, as well as the clouds, could cause the weird shifting of shadows, but still something about it left him uneasy.

City boy, he thought. *Freaking out over the trees' shadows. Man, I gotta get over this.*

Seven

SUNDAY, 11:43 A.M.

The road simply ended. No cul-de-sac. No sign like the ones they had seen before: "PRIVATE PROPERTY. NO TRESPASSING." Or "NO MOTORIZED VEHICLES BEYOND THIS POINT." Just road . . . then trees.

Dad pulled to a stop and looked around. He rolled down the window and listened, as though the house would somehow make itself known. Wind in the trees, nothing more. He picked up the listing page and studied it.

Mom leaned forward to squint through the windshield. "Are you sure this is the right place?" she asked.

Dad nodded.

She reached for the paper, but he was already crunching it into a ball. He tossed it out the window.

She said, "Maybe it's out of sight. With all these trees . . ."

"Nah." He shifted into reverse and backed up. Shifting again, he drove sharply toward the side of the road, then reversed again.

"Three-point turn," he told Xander.

"I *know*. We covered that in—" Xander stopped. He was gazing into the woods and saw a line too straight, something too flat to be natural. "Wait. I think I see it."

"What?" Mom said. "The house?" She looked back at him, then to where he was staring. David and Toria clicked out of their seatbelts and crowded up against him to look.

"I . . . think so," he said. He opened the door and stepped out. Toria nearly tumbled out after him. Dad killed the engine, and they gathered at the end of the road.

"I see it!" David said. He ran into the woods.

"Hey!" Dad called. Too late: David was already gone. All of them plunged in, crunching over pine needles and dead branches.

Twenty paces in, Xander saw it and wondered how they had missed it from the road. It was two stories high, and it was capped by a steeply pitched roof, from which two dormer windows protruded. A covered porch ran the length of the front, casting the entry door and entire lower level in shadows. The supports were ornately carved columns. Occupying the left front corner was a round tower that rose slightly higher than the rest of the house. It wasn't really round, though. It was an octagon, with only five sides showing. At the tip of its tall spire was a black weathervane. As Xander watched, an unfelt breeze made it turn; it squeaked like a mouse caught in an eagle's talons. The exterior paint—whatever color it had once been—had been washed gray by years of weather and neglect. It seemed to Xander to be as much a part of the surrounding forest as the trees themselves.

"Oh, Ed!" Mom exclaimed. "It's a Victorian."

"Pure Queen Anne," Dad agreed.

Tendrils of mist slithered over the forest floor, around the base of trees. Xander noticed that some of it had climbed the porch pillars and drifted, almost invisibly, over the shingles of the porch roof. It reminded him of an old TV series Dean's dad had bought on DVD: *Dark Shadows*. It was about a creepy old house and a vampire who lived there. Barnabas, Xander remembered.

David was standing farther in, halfway to the house. His head was bent back as he took in the tower, tall as a silo.

Mom said, "I think it used to be green, with darker trim."

"Makes sense," Dad suggested. "One of the original tenets of Victorian architecture was that homes blend in with their surroundings."

37

Xander hung back as his family moved forward as one. Something on the ground caught his eye and he stepped over to it. Off to the side, away from where they had walked, shoe prints were pushed into an area of soft dirt. The prints approached the house at an angle. Xander scanned back toward the road, where they came from, then toward the house, but did not see any other prints. He wondered how long ago they had been made. They seemed fresh, undamaged by rain or wind or scampering animals.

The back of his neck tingled and he knew—*knew!*—he was being watched. He spun toward his family, but their attention was on the house. He scanned the windows, expecting to see someone looking out or a curtain falling back in place. But he saw nothing like that: no faces, no moving curtains. The feeling of being watched stayed with him. He thought of Barnabas again and a shiver ran up his spine, like a spider with cold feet.

His family had reached the steps leading up to the porch and double front doors. The wood creaked as they climbed, and Xander half-expected one of them to crash through the rotting boards.

"Is anyone home?" Toria asked.

"I don't think anyone lives here, honey," Mom said.

"Why not?" David said. "It's cool."

Wind blew through the treetops, and the weathervane *squeeeeeeaked.* Xander looked up at it, and it rotated slowly to point at him.

Without knocking, Dad pushed open the door and walked in. Mom followed, then David and Toria. To Xander, it looked like the house was eating them, just popping them in, one at a time.

"Hey!" he called to the open doorway. He felt uneasy but didn't know why. It was just an old house in the woods. And the footprints could have been left by the real estate people or someone else looking for a house. He walked toward the front steps. A breeze blew past him. It was cold, and it came from the house. He looked up at the eaves, where the roof hung over the sides of the house. It looked taller, this close. He had the sense that he had not walked up to the house, but it had walked up to him, a monster sizing him up.

David's voice drifted out to him, saying something was cool.

He ascended the steps. They groaned and creaked. At the open doorway, he stopped. A curved staircase followed the wall to the second floor high above the first. To his right, a wide doorway serviced a dining room. He could see two chairs, part of a table, a buffet, and cabinets on the far wall. The doors pushed straight into the walls—pocket doors, Xander knew they were called. They were what David had thought was cool.

To his left another archway led to a study or library. Its walls were lined in shelves that were packed with dusty books. Straight ahead, beyond the foyer, a hallway led to a room where the family was gathered. From their words, he assumed they were in the kitchen: "Here's a pantry." "Beautiful cabinets . . ." "There are dirty dishes in the sink!" "Gross!"

Furniture, books, dishes in the sink. If the items themselves suggested someone still lived there, the setting quickly corrected that misconception. Cobwebs clung to the corners where the walls and ceiling met. Dust coated the floors, showing where his family had walked as clearly as if they had traipsed over the smooth beach sand. Wallpaper curled off the walls like peels from a banana. Several banister spindles were broken or missing. Grime lined the fancy carvings in the wood on the banister, around the doors, the doors themselves. Gaps wide enough to stick a finger into had formed between several planks in the hardwood floor.

"Xander!" Dad called from the kitchen. He beckoned to him. "Come on! Check this out!"

He stepped fully into the house. The air inside was cool on his skin. He turned, expecting the front door to close on its own. But it stayed open, as it was supposed to. He shook his head, chiding himself for letting an old house spook him. He walked toward the kitchen.

Behind him, the front door slammed shut.

CHAPTER

eight

Xander spun around to stare at the door. It had closed on
its own.

And only after all of us had come in, he thought.

From the kitchen behind him, his dad said, "Isn't this
incredible?"

"Did you see that?" Xander asked, pointing at the door,
but when he stepped into the kitchen, it was empty.

"Whatta ya think?" Dad asked.

Xander turned around to see his father coming toward him from the direction of the front door. His mouth went dry. "Weren't you just in the kitchen?"

"I was. I walked around. You okay?"

"No, I mean . . . yes, but . . ."

His dad tilted his head. "Xander?"

"There's something going on." He was looking past his father to the front door.

"Going on?" Dad asked.

"Something strange. First I heard you in the kitchen, and uh . . ." Xander's head was swimming. "Then the front door slammed . . . by itself."

"It's an old house," his father explained. "Hinges start to sag and that causes doors to close on their own. Have you seen the round room, the one in the tower?"

Xander shook his head.

Mom's voice called down from upstairs. Xander would have sworn she was in the kitchen a few seconds ago as well.

"Dad," Xander said. "Doesn't something about this place seem weird to you?"

"You mean the stuff, the dishes? Whoever lived here before did a poor job packing up, huh?"

"No, I mean *really* weird."

"Like what?"

"Like . . ." Xander didn't know where to start. There was the door shutting after he'd thought about it doing that very thing. His father had chalked it up to sagging hinges. But what about hearing Dad in the kitchen when he was somewhere else? And the chill he'd gotten outside, when he felt as though he was being watched?

"Ed," Mom called again.

"Hold on a sec," his father told Xander, holding up his index finger. He went into the foyer and started up the stairs.

Xander went to the front door and squinted at the hinges. They were dirty and rusty, but otherwise looked fine. The house creaked around Xander. He thought of the way dogs sometimes whimpered when you gave them special attention. He wondered if the house creaked all the time, maybe from constant settling or from the wind buffeting against it . . . or if it was responding to his family's presence. Voices and footsteps streamed at him from the corridors and upper landing. He could identify each voice, but not the direction from which it came. He heard David in the kitchen again, but didn't see anyone in there. Movement caught his eye, and he looked up to the second floor landing. A hallway disappeared to the left and right. Two doors were visible. One was open, and he saw David standing in the threshold, his familiar silhouette backlit by sunlight coming through a window behind him.

"David!" he called.

"What?" David said, almost beside him.

Xander jumped. David was standing at the foot of the stairs, having stepped out of the dining room.

"David!" Xander yelled, because he had to yell something. His eyes snapped back to the figure in the upstairs doorway, but it was gone.

"What do you want?" David asked.

"I . . . were you just upstairs?"

"I haven't looked up there yet."

"But I just saw you up there."

David gave him a funny look. "Not me. Look at this." He stepped closer to show what he held in his hand. At first Xander thought it was a flashlight, and then he recognized it: a toy light-saber. The plastic red tube that represented the laser had broken off, but the cylindrical handle, with its decorative rings and On/Off switch, was unmistakable. It was old.

"Some kid must have lived here a long time ago," David said.

"Or came in to play."

Xander heard excited voices coming from . . . somewhere. "I really love it, Ed. I do," his mom said.

"Even with all the work?"

"Yes, yes. How else could we afford something this big? If we ever got into a house like this, it would have to be a fixer-upper."

His parents were upstairs, but the voices seemed to be drifting from everywhere at once: the library, the kitchen, the second floor. Relief washed over him when they appeared in the upstairs hallway. Mom leaned over the railing. "It's big, boys. Seven bedrooms!"

"Seven?" David said. "What would we do with that many?"

"You can each have your own, for starters," Dad said. "Your mother's counting servants' quarters up here . . ."

"Servants!" David said, tickled at the idea.

"That doesn't mean we're going to *get* any," Dad said. "Besides, that room needs a lot of work, so we can't use it. For now, anyway."

In his excitement, David ran halfway up the stairs. "So, can we live here?"

Dad looked at Mom to answer. "We'll see what we can do."

Xander felt his stomach roll over on itself. He wanted to get out of the house, but he didn't like the idea of going outside alone. He thought of the shoe prints he'd seen. "Dad, can I show you something outside? It might be important."

Dad looked at him curiously. He gave Mom a quick kiss and clomped down the stairs. "What is it?" he asked.

Mom stopped him. "Ed, where's Victoria?" she said with that hint of worry mothers seem capable of conjuring at a moment's notice.

Everything he felt about the house made Xander panic. Instantly, he yelled, "Toria! Toria!"

His dad gave him a puzzled look, then called for his daughter.

Silence. Not even the creaking, which had seemed so loud and constant a few minutes before.

"Toria!" Dad called again. He looked up to Mom.

She said, "I haven't seen her since we came in."

"Check up there," he said. He came the rest of the way down the stairs and turned into the dining room.

Xander went the other direction, through the library. He circled around and met up with Dad in the kitchen. When they returned to the foyer, Mom was coming off the last step, worry and hope etched on her face.

"Not down here," Dad informed her. His voice had risen a notch. He appeared more concerned than Mom now.

"Ed—" she started.

Footsteps came from upstairs, running, growing louder. All of them looked. The footsteps grew closer. *They sound like Toria's,* Xander thought. A little girl's. *Please let it be her.* When the footsteps could not possibly get any closer, she still did not appear, but the pounding continued. Again, Xander glanced toward the dining room, the kitchen, the library. Considering the tricks of sound he had witnessed, he no longer assumed his sister was upstairs. And that was *if* the footsteps belonged to her.

"What in the world . . . ?" his father said.

"I looked up there," Mom assured him. She called, "Victoria!"

Dad went to the stairs. He hesitated, as if fearful of what he would find at the top.

Toria emerged from the shadows of the upstairs hall. She stopped at the railing, all teeth and dimples. "Hey, guys!"

"Where were you?" Mom asked.

Toria looked confused by her tone. She pointed. "In that bedroom, right there."

"But I looked, honey."

"I didn't see you either," Toria said, shrugging. "I think the room used to belong to a little boy."

"See?" David said, slapping Xander's arm with the lightsaber.

Dad said, "Come on down, sweetheart. It's time to go."

"Ahhh," she complained.

"Come on." Dad approached Xander. "What did you want to show me?"

"Nothing, never mind," Xander said. They were leaving anyway, and what would Dad say about shoe prints in the dirt? Exactly what Xander already considered: that they were left by someone looking for a house, just like they were. No biggie.

At the 4Runner, Xander looked around. The house was easy to spot now that he knew it was there, but he could also see how they had missed it the first time. The woods were shadowy and so was the house. He noticed there wasn't any trash caught in the bushes at the edge of the forest. Or beer bottles scattered around. He thought that was funny, since a dead end like this was exactly what high school kids looked for in a party place. Either there were too many dead ends in these backwoods or too few teenagers looking to party. He didn't want his family to be the only litterbugs, so he snatched up the crumpled property listing his father had discarded and pushed it into his pocket.

All the way back to the motel—a good ten minutes, at least—the car buzzed with ideas for making the house their home. Dad said it needed, first and foremost, a thorough cleaning. Mom wanted to paint, recarpet the floors, and stain the wood. Toria knew exactly which bedroom she wanted. And David grumbled about not getting a chance to scope out the upstairs. Only Xander remained silent. If they were really going to live there, he hoped his uneasiness about it went away. He didn't think he could feel this way—all tight inside—24/7.

CHAPTER

nine

Everyone else was asleep except Xander and David. They were lying in bed, facing each other.

"I don't know . . . just a *feeling*, like in . . ." Xander thought for a moment. "*Star Wars.* You know, when Han Solo says, 'I've got a bad feeling about this'?"

"Didn't they *all* say that?" David whispered back. "Luke and Leia and . . ."

"My point is the *feeling*, not who *said* it."

The only light came from a sodium vapor lamp that illuminated the motel parking lot. It slipped in where the curtains didn't quite meet and cut a shimmering line over the boys' bed. It was almost too quiet to sleep. No car horns or sirens. No hum of the city, which you didn't notice until you got away from it. Mom's rhythmic breathing told Xander she was fast asleep. Dad's slumber seemed less peaceful, and he didn't quite snore, but his breathing was loud. Xander imagined lions sounding like that. Toria was a quiet sleeper except for an occasional rolling over. Something in the room ticked: not a clock, but like a car engine cooling down. Or like someone sitting in the corner of the room making noises with his lips.

For an hour Xander had had been listening to the subtle sounds, unable to get the house out of his head. He had tapped David on the shoulder and whispered his name. It had taken several proddings to wake him. Finally, the boy had rolled over to face Xander. Xander had asked him if he had sensed anything weird at the house. David had thought about it. He'd said it was a little creepy but couldn't offer any specifics.

Now, David said, "So what, you don't like the house? You don't want to live there?"

Xander was torn. There was a lot to like about the house: its size, that it was so isolated in the woods, that it *looked* cool.

If they had to live in Hicksville, they could certainly find worse places than that house. But then . . .

"When I was outside, before we went in, it felt like someone was watching me . . . someone *inside* the house," he said.

"You think it's *haunted*?" From the glow of the lamplight, Xander saw David's eyes grow wide.

"I don't know, but you know how in scary movies something is watching somebody or sneaking up on them, and the person feels it?"

David nodded.

"It was like that."

"You're scaring me."

Xander looked at his brother. If scaring him would make David more aware, more sensitive to the house's weirdness, he decided maybe freaking him out was a good thing.

"Remember *Supernatural*, that TV show?"

David nodded. They'd watched it together a few times.

"Those guys face off with vampires and werewolves and ghosts, but they're not afraid, they just do it."

"You think *vampires* live in the house?" The pitch of his voice had risen a notch. He was starting to sound like Toria.

"I'm not saying that." He closed his eyes. He wasn't sure what he was saying, what he wanted. A brother in arms. Someone to validate his unease. He hoped something more would come from waking David than just spooking him. "Listen, just keep your eye out, okay? If you see anything weird, just let me know."

"Weird?" David paused a moment. He said, "You mean, besides you?"

Xander could sense more than see David's smile. He wished he could be more like that, easygoing. But then, David hadn't seen what Xander had seen.

CHAPTER

ten

In the morning, Dad announced he was heading out to talk to the real estate agent about the house.

"Can I come?" Xander asked.

"You're not ready, are you?"

"He hasn't even brushed his teeth," Mom said. She was sitting on the rollaway, brushing Toria's hair.

Dad rolled his eyes at Xander. He gestured toward the door

with his head. He tiptoed to the door and opened it quietly—as if anything could happen secretly in a twenty-by-twenty motel room, never mind the flood of sunlight that opening the door brought in.

Grinning, Xander grabbed his T-shirt, socks, and sneakers and hurried out. As he pulled the door shut, Mom called, "At least get some gum."

In the car, Xander asked, "You didn't notice anything strange about the house?"

Dad took his time to answer. "I think it's a *special* house, Xander. We wouldn't buy it if it weren't."

Xander bristled. Now he knew how it felt to be like Kevin McCarthy in *Invasion of the Body Snatchers*—a person who *knew* something was wrong but was chalked up as crazy because he couldn't prove it. He couldn't even count the number of movies featuring *that* character. If it happened so often on film, it must be pretty common in real life, right? He had the brief image of himself in a white padded room, arms bound by sleeves that tied in the back, yelling through a little window in the door. "I'm not insane, really!" Nurse Ratched would slam the window shut and his cell mate, Jack Nicholson, would tell him to shut up.

He said, "No, I mean—"

"You mean the sounds?" his father asked.

Hope flared in Xander's gut, feeling a little like when a roller coaster reaches the peak of a tall climb. "Yeah! The *sounds.*"

"I think all that creaking and groaning was just the house settling, or getting used to having people in it again."

The roller coaster stalled. "Yeah, settling."

Dad cleared his throat. Xander noticed the skin on his forehead and around his eyes wrinkle in thought. Dad said, "And the way the sounds seem to trick you."

Back on the coaster. Xander smiled. "You noticed that?"

His dad threw him a glance. "Of course. I mean, how many footsteps could Toria have taken to get from one end of the house to the other? It's big, but with all that noise, you'd have thought she was running in place."

Xander hadn't considered that. If that had been the only trick of sound, he might have been able to accept that explanation. He could tell his dad didn't buy it either. "What about . . . *other* things? Like noises coming from a different direction than they should have?"

For a moment, Dad was unreadable. Xander waited like a man for a verdict. Finally, Dad nodded. "That too," he said quietly.

Xander felt tension fall away from his chest like a bandage that had been constricting his lungs. The way his dad had said it was all he needed to know: there *was* something weird about the house. Something that had made his father uneasy as well. And if the house's strangeness revealed itself through sound, then why not visually too? How Dad had appeared to move instantly from one side of the house to the other, the silhouette that had looked like David in the doorway upstairs.

Weren't these just the eyeball equivalent of the tricks on his ears?

"Why is it like that?" he asked.

"I don't know, Son. I really don't."

"But . . . doesn't it *bother* you?" Obviously not, since they were heading to a real estate agent to buy the place.

Dad smiled at Xander. "Not yet."

CHAPTER

eleven

Kathy Bates, Xander thought. Not the homicidal loony from *Misery* but the little-too-happy, bubbly Bates from *Rat Race.* That's who the real estate woman reminded him of. Like Bates, there was plenty of her. She seemed to find everything funny regardless of who said it or how unfunny it was.

"Ooh . . . you just rolled in from Pasadena!" She laughed —her whimsy at the use of the word *rolled* or at Pasadena,

Xander couldn't tell. "And you're looking for a house?"

Mr. King smiled, the way people do when they're waiting for a punchline. "Well, actually, I think we found one."

"Just go ahead and make my job easy, will ya?" she said and lowered herself into the chair behind the office space's single desk. She positioned a keyboard in front of her and said, "Which one?"

"At the end of Gabriel Road."

She looked up and somehow kept her smile while forming a perplexed expression. "Off of Highway 3 . . . and Rem Way?"

A bulge the size of Xander's thumb appeared between her eyes. "I don't think . . ." She started typing, squinting at the monitor. Xander turned to look out the big front window. Across the street was some kind of lumber mill. Whole trees, stripped of branches and bark, were piled into stacks the size of office buildings. Someone was using a fire hose to spray water over the logs. Perhaps it was to keep them from burning up at the slightest spark. It didn't look safe to Xander.

A paper cup tumbled by in the parking lot, and Xander remembered. He pushed his hand into his pocket and pulled out the crumpled property listing his father had tossed away. It was exactly what Kathy Bates needed. He unfolded it and smoothed out the wrinkles. But this wasn't the house on Gabriel Road. The picture was of a smallish cabin they had not seen. Dad had tossed it out the window, frustrated that it had led him to nowhere. That was before Xander had seen the house in the shadows. *Could Dad have been looking at the wrong property listing?* he wondered. If so, how had they found the house?

Another thought occurred to him, and it chilled his skin. What if the house's power was so strong it made Dad see something on the page that wasn't there? Or maybe it had even changed the page after getting them there.

That's called paranoia, Xander thought. *Stop it!*

He crunched the paper back into a ball. He tossed it into a wastebasket by the desk.

"There's nothing here. I'm sorry," Kathy Bates said. Then something dawned on her. "You're talking about the old Konig place!"

"Konig?" his father said. He glanced at Xander.

"That ol' rundown place?" she laughed. "I didn't know it was for sale. Was there a sign?"

"No, but . . ."

Xander said, "There was a property listing."

"Really?" She squinted at him as though he had just said his name was Johnny Depp.

"Off the Internet," his father said. "I think it was your Web site."

She shook her head. "Not mine. Not if that property was listed. But then we all share the same listing service, so I don't know . . ."

"Is it for sale?" Dad asked.

She laughed. "Well, my daddy used to say everything is for sale. Let me look into it." She looked at Xander, then back to Dad. "It's pretty rundown, you know. Nobody's lived there for . . . I don't know, thirty or forty years. Way before my time." She leaned over her desk—as much as she possibly could—and whispered, "The man who lived there . . ." She looked again at Xander. "Well, I shouldn't say."

Dad turned to leave.

Xander knew he had no patience for rumors. Xander had no such qualms. He said, "What about him, the man who used to live there?"

Happy to have Xander's ear, she said, "They say he killed his wife."

Xander took a step back. He threw a shocked expression at Dad, who had turned back, interested.

"Schoolteacher. Just disappeared. After the authorities started asking questions, the man and the rest of his family vanished."

"Family?" Xander said.

"Little boy and girl. I don't know how old. Sweetest family in the world, if you listen to the old folks around here."

Xander was stunned. "And nobody knows what happened to them?"

"Some say they high-tailed it to Europe." She raised her eyebrows at him. "Most believe he took them somewhere and killed them. Then took his own life."

Dad forced a smile. "Just old rumors," he said. "Thank you for looking into this for us. I'll be back." He strode for the door.

Xander's feet felt like cement. He didn't like that a house he already thought had problems also had a gruesome history. He knew it shouldn't have surprised him. Every haunted house in every movie he had ever seen got that way by some tragic event in the past. He wanted to ask the woman what else she knew, but his dad had already pushed through the door. He nodded at her inquisitive look and hustled to catch up.

twelve

MONDAY, 11:27 P.M.

"It *is* haunted."

Night again. The same swath of lamplight stole through the curtains. The same parental breathing. That *tick tick tick* lip sound.

"What do you mean?" David squirmed under the covers.

"That toy you found? The lightsaber? It belonged to a little boy. His father killed the whole family."

David's eyes got huge, then flickered as he thought about that.

"It's like *The Shining*," Xander continued. "The hotel drove the dad crazy."

"How do you know?"

"I saw the movie."

"No. How do you know about the family, the dad who killed them?"

"The real estate lady told us. They never found any of them."

"And it's *haunted*?"

"Has to be. Look, weird things were happening there and—"

"What weird things?"

Xander hadn't told David everything. "Just some stuff. But I told you I got a bad feeling about it, then we find out about this murder." He emphasized it: "A *triple* murder and suicide. A guy *slaughtered* his own family. How awful is that?"

"*Slaughtered*? What'd he do?"

"I'm sure it was something bloody and grotesque. You don't go out of your mind and keep it neat."

Xander could almost see the vivid images bouncing around David's head.

"What do we do?" David asked.

Good question.

"Do you still want to move into that house?"

"Not if it's haunted!"

"Shhhh." Against reason, Xander still felt the *thrill* he had experienced at the house. That sense of adventure, that he was privy to some kind of secret knowledge. He imagined finding another house, one without a history or ghosts. Yeah, he'd sleep better at night, but he'd be bored out of his mind during the day. Especially in Pinedale.

"Look," Xander said. "Let's just keep our eyes open, be really watchful. If it gets dangerous, we'll go nuts—you know, scream and throw a fit or something—to get everybody out."

"I can do that." David smiled, but his eyes said he was still worried.

•••••••••

The next day, they looked at more properties, but their hearts weren't in the search, and they saw nothing they liked.

The following day, Wednesday, Mr. King pulled to the curb in front of Tall Pines Park. The boys, Toria, and Mom had staked a claim at one of the picnic tables. They'd walked from the motel to the park, stopping at a burger joint on the way. Xander and David had already devoured their fries, but Mom had made them wait for their cheeseburgers until Dad showed up.

Their father did a sort of half-skip across the grass. His smile showed where Toria and David got their dimples; Mom and Xander had radiant smiles without them—at least that's what Mom said.

Dad stopped at the head of the table. "Well," he said, "it's ours."

"The house?" David squealed. "I mean *the* house?"

"We haven't closed, of course, but the trust that owns it has agreed to a price and said we can move in right away, if we want."

Mom nodded. Xander realized she had known all along, but she'd kept it a surprise.

Dad leaned down to give her a big kiss. Xander and David exchanged a look, one with equal parts happiness and fear. Xander thought if you took a picture of them during a really scary part of a really good movie, they would look like they did now. He hoped he was right about the house being more frightening than dangerous, and he wondered, if he was wrong, if they would realize it before someone got hurt.

"So what do you say?" Dad clapped his hands. "Want to go to our new home?"

"Now?" Toria said.

"Sure." He saw Xander and David eyeing their burgers. "Bring 'em; we'll have a picnic there."

●●●●●●●●

Xander hadn't thought about it until now, but it was odd pulling up to their home when the only things visible were trees. There was no driveway, no garage. Who would build a home like that? At least in this age of mass transit. It made him wonder how old the house was, who had designed it, who had built it, who had lived in it.

Dad stopped where the road did. He must have been thinking similar thoughts, for he said, "There's not even a curb to pull over to. I wonder if building a carport or a drive up to the house would be too expensive."

"I don't mind parking here," Mom said.

"Wait till it rains," David said, and laughed.

Mom laid her hand on Dad's arm. "Besides, I have a feeling this house is going to take everything we have."

That made Xander shudder. He opened the door, appreciative of the sun.

David carried the food. Mom had a blanket. As they approached the house, Xander thought about how he and David would begin the inspection as soon as they were settled in. He knew the best way to unearth the house's secrets was to have an open mind. In the movies, too many people missed important clues because they were looking for something else, some preconceived notion of what they would find. Even with this in mind, he couldn't help but think they might locate the bodies of the family who had disappeared. Most screenwriters these days would have them buried in the basement. But Xander liked the old Edgar Allen Poe stories like "The Black Cat" in which people were bricked-up in walls. Not always *after* being murdered.

Dad, Mom, and Toria tromped up the front steps. Dad swung the door open with a "Ta-da."

Mom said, "We'd better get a locksmith out here, first thing."

"Already taken care of," Dad said. "I called him from the car on the way to the park."

They streamed in. Xander stood at the bottom of the steps, his foot on the first one. David tested the banister's strength, then leaned against it. "Xander," he whispered. "'Member what we were talking about? About the place being haunted?"

Xander stepped closer. "Shhh."

"I can *feel* it." He said, "Can we share a room? Just for a while?"

Xander smiled. He was glad David had suggested it first. Now he had to be careful about appearing overeager. "Let's see how it goes."

"Okay, but . . ." David's voice trailed off, and he bowed his head.

"But?"

"I don't think I can stay here if I have to sleep alone."

"There's always Toria," Xander suggested.

David made a face. "That would be *worse*."

"Than *what*? Getting eaten by vampires?" Xander started up the steps.

"Don't say that!" David moved in close to him.

"I'm just kidding, David. Don't worry about it." They

stopped at the open door. Dust moats drifted in the gloom. They were catching the sunlight and were bright as stars in a black galaxy. The others were out of sight; their voices drifted out to Xander. They were obviously talking to one another, but now it didn't surprise Xander that they seemed to come from different places in the house and from different distances away. Standing next to him, David found his hand and gripped it. He looked at his little brother, who offered no other sign of fear.

"Besides," David said, "vampires don't *eat* you. They drink your blood."

Xander thought about responding with something wise like, "Those are normal vampires; this house has a different breed." But he figured he had scared David enough—had scared *himself* enough. So instead, he said, "Fine, Dr. Van Helsing. You're the expert." And with that, they stepped into the house together.

CHAPTER

thirteen

Victoria told everyone she wanted the room that had been decorated for a little boy, even though the one across and a bit down the hall from it had obviously belonged to a little girl. "Too pink," she called it.

"Should we let her pick *either* of them?" David whispered.

"Why not?" Xander asked.

"The little boy and the little girl?" David said, as though speaking to an imbecile.

"So?"

"They were *murdered*. What if their ghosts still think those are their rooms?"

Xander shook his head. "You're worrying too much. Just watch out for anything weird. Don't let your imagination get ahead of you."

"You sound like Dad."

Xander accepted that. "Which room do you want?"

"Not one of those. What room do *you* want? It's going to be *our* room, isn't it?"

Xander stood tall, stretching his spine. Maybe sharing a room for a while wasn't such a bad idea. As they got used to the house, and as they discovered—as they probably would—that it wasn't haunted, Xander could move into a room of his own. He patted his brother on the chest. "All right. Yeah. Sure. As long as I can put my posters on the wall."

"Not *Friday the 13th*."

"No scary ones," Xander agreed. He gestured with his head. "Let's look down here."

They moved farther away from the central staircase, past the murdered boy's room.

No, no, no, he thought, *don't start that. Simply, the boy's room.*

He stopped at the door to what used to be a little girl's room. He nudged it open. It creaked into a shadow-filled room. Faint light came through two dirty windows and thin curtains—Mom had called them sheers—that may have been white at one time. There was an old dresser and a bed with a canopy. Didn't matter: Dad had said they would not sleep on any beds or bedding found here anyway. They were probably dirty and had bedbugs.

David said, "Toria's right: too pink. Let's keep looking."

The next room was dingy, dusty, and dark. Nothing about it appealed to either boy.

They moved to the next door which served the corner room on the front side of the house. Xander pushed it open, and they took a step in. This room had a chest of drawers against the far wall and a bed with a simple wooden headboard. Like the other room, two dirty windows let in meager light. The coolest part of the room was that one corner opened up into the tower, a five-sided room-within-a-room. Heavy curtains covered the tower windows, except for the center one, which—

Someone was standing in front of it.

Backlit by the window, the figure was nothing more than a black silhouette to Xander's eyes. David had spotted the shape as well. His hand found Xander's again and squeezed painfully. Xander realized both of them had stopped breathing. The only sound was the figure's labored breath, deep and heavy. The thing shifted. Its head appeared to turn toward them. When it spoke, its voice was baritone and gravelly: "Come in, boys."

David screamed first. It was long and high pitched. Xander's quick "Ahhh!" was almost completely lost in the sound of

David's fear. They turned together and knocked each other into the door frame. They were almost into the hall when they heard a familiar voice call their names. They were through the doorway and moving in separate directions, when they heard, "Boys! Boys! Come back!" and uncontrollable laughter.

Xander stopped and looked back. David had stopped as well, halfway through the doorway at the end of the hall. The boy's eyes were saucers of shock.

From the room: "Xander! David!"

They scowled at each other. Xander took a cautious step toward the door.

Dad stepped into the hallway between them. He looked at Xander, then at David. He said, "Sorry. Really." He stifled a laugh.

David, generally calm, cool, and collected, yelled at the top of his lungs, "That's not funny!"

Dad walked toward him. "I know, I know. I'm sorry. I couldn't help myself." He hugged his youngest son, who resisted, then gave in. He looked back at Xander with a guilty smile.

Xander shook his head and pointed at David. "What *he* said."

Dad nodded. "You guys have been whispering about this house since we talked to the real estate woman. I couldn't resist."

The muscles in Xander's face felt tight. He said, "You know what they say about payback."

Dad snickered. He said, "My boys, my brave young men."

Still pressed against him, David punched his father in the side.

Dad let out an exaggerated grunt and pushed back from him. "So," he said, "have you picked out a room?"

"We're *trying*," David said. "What about beds?"

"Your old beds will be here in a few days. I just have to tell the moving company we found a place."

"And till then?"

"We'll stay in the motel."

"Not here?" Xander asked.

Dad shook his head. "We have to do some cleaning first, get the utilities turned on, make sure everything's safe."

As if to punctuate his last word, Mom yelled, "Ed! Ed!" All three of them looked one way, then the other. It was impossible to tell where she was. Dad made a decision and ran toward the main staircase. Xander and David followed. Toria came out of her room, knocking David against the wall. They clambered down the stairs together. Dad stepped into the foyer, looked down the corridor to the kitchen, and called, "G!"

Her voice came back with an edge of panic: "Ed!"

He started for the kitchen. Xander stopped him. "Dad, in here."

Mom stood in the dining room near one of the windows. Dad pushed past the kids to reach her. "Are you all right? What's wrong?"

She pointed. Dust covered the floors. Most of it had been

75

disturbed by their own shuffling around. Near the walls, in corners, under furniture, it had remained thick and as unbroken as an arctic landscape. Here, in such a spot, were two footprints. They were from bare feet twice the size of Dad's. The toes were pointed toward the window, as though someone had stood there, watching.

CHAPTER

fourteen

They were sitting at a big, round table in the café. Each of them leaned in toward the center.

"The door was unlocked," Dad whispered. "That's how *we* got in. Who knows how long the house had been open to anyone who tried the front door?"

"Or how long ago those footprints were made," Mom added.

"Mom," Xander said, "they were *fresh*. There was no dust in them, just bare wood."

"They were so big," David said.

"It was Bigfoot," Toria said, with a hint of danger.

"Toria," Xander said.

"Well, it was somebody with really big feet," Mom said, "but I don't think it was Bigfoot, honey. Not *the* Bigfoot."

"But he lives here," Toria said. "I read about it."

"Bigfoot's not real," David said.

"Is too."

"Okay, okay. Whether it was a guy with big feet or it was Bigfoot, doesn't really matter, I don't want him in my house. So, listen . . ."

The waitress stepped up behind Toria. She smiled inquisitively, taking in their conspiratorial postures. "Ya ready?"

Dad smiled apologetically. "Not yet. But how about waters all around?"

"Gotcha," she said and wandered away.

All faces turned back to Dad.

He said, "Tomorrow we all go over there and start cleaning. Xander and I will go through the whole house. Basement to attic. We'll see if anybody's there."

Toria inhaled sharply and covered her mouth. *A bit melodramatic,* Xander thought, but that was Toria.

"Or if there are ways to get in we don't know about," Dad said.

David said, "I want to search too."

Dad shook his head. "I don't think—"

Xander touched Dad's arm and said, "He can do it."

Dad studied Xander's face. Maybe he was trying to gauge whether Xander was sticking up for his brother because he thought David could handle it, or because he was going to use the opportunity to somehow scare Dae. Whatever he saw in Xander's eyes, he seemed to appreciate it. He nodded, said, "Okay. It'll be the King boys then."

David smiled. "And may God have mercy on anyone we find . . ."

"Because *we* won't!" Xander finished.

•••••• ••

THURSDAY, 10:49 A.M.

The flashlight beams pushed away the inky blackness of the basement. The walls and floor were stone. Cobwebs and spiderwebs everywhere. David pointed out that he heard the squeaking of rodents and the click of their claws on the stone. "I don't like this," he said.

"No kidding," Xander said.

Dad said, "We'll just take a walk around. See if there's anything obvious. We don't have to move things around, or anything."

What they had seen so far was a basement full of wooden crates, loose lumber, and cardboard boxes that had mostly rotted away,

79

spilling their contents of old clothes, dishes, and record albums onto the floor. The electricity was supposed to have been turned on, but it hadn't been when Dad last checked. It was impossible to tell how large the basement was. Their lights did not go far, and the area was divided by stone walls that seemed to Xander to be haphazardly placed. If it occupied the same square footage as the first floor, it would be big enough to install an Olympic-sized pool or maybe a couple bowling alleys.

"So what are we looking for?" David asked.

Dad said, "Evidence that someone is squatting down here."

"Squatting? Gross," David said.

Xander laughed.

"It means living somewhere you're not supposed to," Dad explained.

"Or *doing* something you're not supposed to," David said.

This time they all laughed. Their voices seemed to cut away some of the gloom. It made the search less creepy. Their flashlights came upon a wood-plank door. Xander and David looked to Dad.

"Let's check all the rooms. Keep your eyes open for doors or recesses that might lead to a sub-basement or root cellar or to the outside."

"This is like a video game," David said.

"It's like *And Then There Were None*," Xander corrected. "That's where all these people are stuck in a house and they're—"

"That's enough, Xander," Dad said.

They stood with their flashlights on the door. No one moved.

If Xander were directing this, he would have a camera approaching them from behind while they weren't looking. He spun around, panning the light back and forth.

"What?" David said, a little too shrill.

"Nothing. Thought I heard something."

No one moved toward the door. Xander said, "Dad?"

"All right." He moved to the door. Xander's heart leaped as a black figure sprung up in front of Dad. Then he realized it was Dad's shadow. Xander's and David's flashlights had created it. Dad pulled open the door. Its hinges squealed like a rat caught in a trap.

"And don't scare us," David said in a loud whisper.

Dad's light moved around the room, then he stepped back. He shut the door. "Nothing," he said. "And how about this . . ." He used his finger to draw a big cartoon face in the dust on the door. the figure's name was "Bob," and Dad had been drawing him since he'd been a kid. Bob was the family's unofficial mascot.

When he finished, Dad smiled and nodded. "There. Now we've marked this area as ours."

"I can think of another way to mark our territory," Xander said.

"Hey," Dad said. "None of that."

Together they moved through the basement, checking rooms and corners. They saw lots of spiders and rat poop, dust and dirt, but no people or indications that someone had ever lived down there. When the stairs came back around, Xander sighed with relief.

"What do the cops say?" Dad asked.

"Clear!" Xander called.

"All right, then," Dad said. "Onward and upward." He climbed the stairs, clicking his flashlight off as he neared the open door at the top.

"No *squatters*," Xander said, making the word sound as gross as he could.

David smiled and started up the stairs. "So what about *And Then There Were None?*" he said.

Xander thought again of the camera moving in the darkness toward him, and he bolted up the stairs right into David's back. "I'll tell you later. Just hurry it up."

CHAPTER

fifteen

They'd gotten through half of the first floor when Mom
called them to lunch. PB&J and potato chips in the dining
room. She had cleaned the room well, and Xander was starting to see the house's potential as a nice home. Even the table
and chairs, left there by the previous owner, had been polished
to a nice shine. They didn't look nearly as battered and ruined
as when Xander had first seen them. Dad said the hardwood

floor needed resurfacing, but it looked fine to Xander, kind of rustic and retro.

"Have you been helping your mom, young lady?" Dad asked Toria.

"I cleaned the windowsills," she said proudly.

"That's it?" David asked.

"And my room!"

Mom nodded. "Mostly, she's been in her room." She handed Dad a paper plate with a sandwich cut diagonally. "I take it you haven't found anyone lurking in our house."

"No squatters," David said and broke up laughing.

Mom gave him a puzzled look.

Smiling, Xander shook his head to show that, at least in front of his mother, he was above such childish humor. He said, "We searched the whole basement."

"Talk about creepy," David said.

"Yeah," Xander agreed, "but we didn't find anybody."

"And no place where anybody's been staying," Dad added. "Or any way to get into the house."

Nonetheless, Mom looked worried. She said, "Could we put a lock on the basement door? Just in case?"

"Sure," Dad said. "We can bolt this place up like Fort Knox." He popped a chip into his mouth.

"We're about half-finished with this floor," Xander said.

Around a mouthful of sandwich, David said, "We're even looking in the closets and cupboards."

"Like anybody would hide in a *cupboard*," Xander said, glaring at Dad.

Dad shrugged. "Never know."

"Lots of gross stuff," David said.

Mom made a face. "Gross stuff?"

Dad said, "Just grime and trash. Stuff like that."

"Rat poop!" David said.

"Eeewww!" Toria said. "I'm not hungry anymore." Xander got an image of her as a mom.

"Rats?" Mom said.

"More like mice," Dad said. "I'll set some traps this afternoon."

"And spiders," David said.

"David, stop. You're scaring Toria," Dad said. To the King ladies he said, "There are not as many spiders as you'd think for a house abandoned so long and in the woods. We'll bug-bomb tonight when we leave."

"Cool!" David said.

"They're not *real* bombs," Xander told him.

David frowned. "Oh."

"They're still cool." Dad raised his eyebrows at David. "Lots of smoke. You can help me."

David nodded. He was pushing an entire half sandwich into his mouth.

Mom surveyed her family, sitting around the table in their new home. "Well, guys," she said, smiling, "think we found our dream house?"

"Yeah!" Toria chimed.

Mouth full of sandwich, David said something indiscernible.

Xander scowled at him. "What?"

He held up a finger, swallowing painfully. "I said . . . we're the Dreamhouse Kings!"

Mom laughed. "I like it. The Dreamhouse Kings." Her eyebrows shot up as she remembered something. Pointing to Dad, she said, "Honey, don't forget your appointment."

Dad stopped chewing; his eyes went wide. He looked at his watch. He swallowed, said, "You boys continue without me. I'm meeting the district superintendent at the school. School starts next Monday, and I haven't even toured the place."

Mom laughed. "Not to mention that you haven't met the teachers, set up your office, reviewed the school calendar—"

"I know, I know," Dad said. He shrugged. "When they hired me I told them I didn't have time to do everything. They said not to worry about it." He smiled. "Getting someone of my caliber is worth a little disorganization. That's what they said."

Mom *aaahhh*'ed. "How sweet."

"So what, you want us to look for intruders *alone?*" Xander asked.

"You'll be fine," he said, glancing at his watch again. He stood. "I have to run by the motel, take a shower, and change." He grabbed the rest of his sandwich and hurried out.

•••••••••

The sun had crested in the sky and started its descent toward the horizon by the time Xander and David brought their inspection to the second floor.

"This is great," David said. "We wanted to search the house anyway. Now we got Dad's help, and we don't have to sneak around. I hope he's back before we get to the attic. I don't want to go up there alone."

"Hey! You're not alone."

"You know what I mean."

"Let's start with the far bedrooms and work our way back," Xander suggested.

As they walked the corridor, their heads swiveled back and forth to look into each room they passed. Toria's bedroom had been swept and the windows washed. It was amazing how much light came in now that the filth was off the glass. It would be even better when they finally got to cleaning the outside.

"Shaping up," David said.

They passed the pink room and the bedroom that was going to be theirs—the corner room with the tower. *Duh.* They hadn't had a chance to do anything with it yet. It was as gloomy as ever.

"Lot left to do," Xander said.

"Yeah, but we haven't found any graves or coffins with vampires or anything like that. I was thinking the basement would be the place for those things."

They stopped outside the open door of the last room on the other side of the hall. Looking back, Xander was struck by how long the corridor really was. It continued beyond the foyer and grand staircase. All told, it was fifty feet, maybe longer. Even then, the far end of the hall bent into another corridor that led only to what Mom and Dad called "the servants' quarters." Xander would have called it a second master bedroom, because it had a walk-in closet and a private bathroom. He thought servants should also have their own kitchenette so they had privacy on their days off; that room didn't have a kitchenette. Still, he hoped it was inhabitable by the time Dae was ready for his own room—Xander would love to claim the "servants' quarters" for himself.

He said, "I don't know. I get the feeling there's more to this house than it's showing us."

They went into the bedroom and flipped on their flashlights. More of the same: dust, old furniture, peeling wallpaper.

"Hey, look at this," Xander said. His light had captured a framed picture on a nightstand. The photograph was faded, almost white, the faces indistinct. But Xander could tell it had once been a color portrait of a family: a man and woman, a little girl whose size would have made her three or four years old, and a blond-haired boy, a few years older.

"Is that the family who was murdered?" David whispered almost reverently.

"I bet." He was thinking how the fading of the photograph made them look like ghosts. In *The Picture of Dorian Gray*, a painting of a man changed to reflect the ravages of his evil deeds instead of reflecting the person himself. It seemed to Xander this picture instead continued to show the reality of the family: faded from the earth, faded from memory. His heart ached for them, for the people they never became. Even the dad, who had done the dirty deed. If the house had gotten to him, was anything he did after that his fault? Wouldn't it be like being hypnotized and forced to do something against your will? Xander resolved again to be alert against the house's power. His family would not suffer the fate of that family. He would not let them fade away.

"Weird they left so many personal things," David said.

"But not everything," Xander said. "Like they left in a hurry."

"If the father murdered them, why would they take anything at all?"

"Maybe they were trying to get away from the house. Maybe it was the police who took their clothes and stuff. Evidence."

David went to a closet. He opened the door and flashed his light inside. "Hey, what's this?" he said.

Leaning into one of the corners was a wood pole, similar to a broom handle. One end had a brass cap with a small hook coming off it.

"I don't know . . . wait a minute, yes, I do." Xander swept the light over the ceiling. He stopped on a rectangular hatch. "The attic entrance. That pole hooks the door and pulls it down. I saw it in a movie."

"We should wait for Dad," David said. "He'd want to come."

Xander smiled. "He'd want to, or you'd want him to?"

David stared at the door for a long time. Finally, he said, "I'm all right."

"Okay, then. Come on."

CHAPTER

Sixteen

It was a bust. The attic turned out to be nothing but dust, mouse poop, spiderwebs, some decomposing cardboard boxes of disintegrated clothes like in the basement, and a few pieces of furniture. They opened a wooden chest, big enough for a man to fit inside, but it was just full of papers—a child's schoolwork, sheet music, stuff like that. They cautiously approached a large wardrobe—definitely where Xander would have hidden if he were a creepy guy hiding in someone else's house. But it contained only a dress and some other clothes on wooden hangers. The space up there was smaller than the other floors, probably having to do with the way the roof canted inward, he figured.

Xander was glad to have cleared the attic without relying on his father. He was also relieved they hadn't uncovered some crazy maniac living up there . . . relieved and a little disappointed. *That* would have been something to call his best friend, Dean, about. Danielle too.

They clambered down the hatch's built-in steps, then used the pole to shove the whole thing back into place. David reached up and slapped at Xander's hair and shoulders. Clouds of dust billowed off him. Xander returned the favor, then said, "Let's check our bedroom. Maybe we can clear the whole house before Dad gets home."

"That'd be cool," David agreed.

Heading to their room, Xander pointed his beam at a narrow door in the corridor wall.

"Check the linen closet," he told David and stepped into the bedroom. Corners, closet, tower: nothing, nothing, nothing. At least no intruders or hidey-holes. In the closet, he did find a garment draped over a wire hanger.

"David," he called over his shoulder, "check under the bed."

He stepped farther into the closet to examine the clothes. It appeared to be a man's suit. Old-fashioned with wide lapels and pinstripes. He remembered something like it from the movie *Bugsy.* A zoot suit, it was called. He tapped it with the end of his flashlight, igniting a small explosion of dust from the fabric. He coughed and waved his hand in front of his face. He left the closet and shut the door. Scanning the room, his brother was nowhere in sight.

"David! Where are you, dude?" He bent and flashed the light under the bed, but David wasn't hiding there. Back in the hallway, he opened the linen closet door. It was narrow and deep. The shelves started a few feet in, leaving a space for maybe brooms or a mop bucket in front of them. His eyes went from the floor to the top shelf. Empty. He shut the door.

"David!" he yelled again. His voice echoed, then cut short, as though whatever messed with the sounds had rippled past, snagging his call. A third time, he yelled for his brother. He flashed his light into the room they had checked first. Letting out a deep sigh, he entered and opened the closet door. Again, nothing. Back in the hallway, he yelled, "David, this isn't funny. Remember how you felt when Dad scared us? Don't mess around."

His voice came back to him: *Don't mess around.* Oh, now the auditory tricks were getting outright scary. From up the hall, his own voice barked out again: *Don't mess around.* His stomach was tightening. He didn't know whether to stand still, look for David, or run like a madman to the front door.

Twenty feet away, a figure stepped out of a bedroom.

"David?" Xander whispered.

93

"Don't mess around," the figure said in Xander's voice and stepped closer.

It was Toria, with that blasted bear in her arms. She squeezed its paw, and it said, "Don't mess around."

"*Victoria!*" Xander yelled, stomping toward her. "Stop that! Where's David?"

"I haven't seen him," she said, frightened by his anger.

"Go back in your room. Stop messing with that bear. I mean it." He followed her into her room, checked the closet, and then he realized: one of the second floor's three bathrooms was between here and the end of the hall. He hurried to it and knocked on the closed door. "David, are you in there? Didn't you hear me calling?" He knocked again, then tried the handle. It was unlocked, the bathroom empty.

Now, not only his stomach felt constricted, but his heart.

"David!" he screamed with everything he had. He ran to the nearest door, the bedroom they would make their own.

Let him be here. Let him be here. Just lost in imagining what our room would be like.

But it was empty. And the closet was empty.

His mom yelled up from below: "Xander, what is it? Is everything all right? Is Dae with you?"

Xander surged into the hall, intent on getting Mom's help. Whether she would blame him for losing his brother didn't matter now.

Movement in the corner of his vision. He looked. David

was standing in the hall, back by the first rooms they had checked. A gash above his eyebrow trickled blood. He looked dazed.

"Xander?" Mom called. Her footsteps clopped on the stairs.

Xander called over his shoulder. "Got it, Mom! Everything's okay!"

"David's okay?"

"Yeah! Just . . . uh . . . bathroom."

Her footsteps descended, echoed in the foyer, and were gone.

Xander rushed to David. "Where were you? What happened?"

"You won't believe me if I tell you."

"Dae, what happened?"

He prodded the cut on his brother's forehead.

David flinched away. He touched it himself, looked at the blood on his fingertips. "Whoa," he said.

Xander had David's blood on his fingers as well. It frightened Xander more than a simple bonk on the head should have. "David—" he began.

David grabbed Xander's arms. "I mean it, you wouldn't believe me if I told you."

"You gotta—"

"I'll *show* you!"

"Show me what?"

"Come on." David opened the linen closet door.

"Were you hiding?" Xander said. "I checked in there."

"Shhh. Just go." He pushed on Xander's back, trying to get him in the closet.

Xander resisted, sidestepped away. "What are you *doing*? I'm not going in there."

David let out an exasperated breath. "I was going to scare you. I went in there and closed the door."

"I told you I looked."

"Something happened. I went somewhere."

"Where?"

"Just go. Please?"

Xander looked from his brother to the closet. He shook his head. "This is some kind of trick."

David's eyes got big. "It *is*! But not like you're thinking. Do it!" When he realized Xander wasn't budging, he said, "Okay. Just do what I do. Promise?"

Xander closed his eyes. "Okay, okay."

David stepped into the closet and turned around. He pulled the door partially shut, said, "Do what I'm doing exactly." He shut the door.

Xander waited. "Okay?" he said to the door. "David?" He opened the door. His brother was gone.

Seventeen

THURSDAY, 2:36 P.M.

The closet shelves were empty. The walls seemed intact. The ceiling and floor showed no sign of harboring a vent or door. David was just gone. There one second, not there the next.

Xander stepped in and felt the shelves. They were solidly mounted. He poked at the walls, on the sides, and behind the shelves. They felt firm and unmoving. "David," he called. He sighed. "All right, I'm doing exactly what you did."

He pulled the door completely closed. Blackness engulfed him. The floor seemed to move as though the closet were an elevator. But his stomach didn't lurch the way it did on elevators. A wind swirled around him and was gone. He felt dizzy. Someone wrapped his arms around him and squeezed. "David?" he said.

But then he realized it wasn't a *someone*. The walls of the closet had squeezed in, becoming so narrow he had to turn sideways. Slits appeared in the closet door. Level with his eyes. Light poured in, blinding him.

"David!" he yelled, panicked now. He pushed against a side wall. It flexed a little and made a metallic popping sound. He pushed his behind into the back wall. The same kind of flexing. The same sound. He pushed his palm into the front door. It felt like cold metal. "David!" he screamed again.

A metallic *click* and *thunk*. The door opened, but its width was now no more than eighteen inches. David stood smiling, holding the door, a step below him. Beyond David, sunlight came in from huge windows. This was *not* the second-floor hallway. He peered around. He was standing in something like a metal coffin. A coat hook almost snagged a nostril.

"What's going on?" he said to David. "Where are we?"

"Step out and look."

Xander squeezed through the metal threshold and stepped down to a tiled floor. He was standing in a short corridor. To his right, the corridor met another, wider hallway, which disappeared around a corner. He walked to the corner. Windows lined one wall running the length of the hallway. What lay beyond seemed familiar to Xander, but he couldn't immediately place it. He turned to see what he had just emerged from. It was a locker, one of a series that occupied the entire wall. They were all painted bright blue.

He said, "What the—"

"We're in the school!" David said.

"What school?"

"Our school. The one we're going to next week."

Xander recognized it now. Outside the windows was the school's yard of lush grass and picnic tables. Beyond that, the parking lot. In fact, Xander realized, their 4Runner was in one of the slots. He pushed his face close to David's and whispered, "Dad's here."

"What do we do?" David asked.

Xander smiled. "Let's look around." He walked back to the locker and shut the door. "Remember this number. One-nineteen." That made him think of something. He asked David, "That *is* how you got back, right? Through the locker?"

"Yeah, that's how I got this." He pointed to the gash above his eyebrow.

The two of them rounded the corner and headed toward a set of double doors at the far end. Every forty feet or so, the lockers gave way to windowed classroom doors. The lights were off in each one. Soon, the place would be full of kids and teachers with hardly a moment of inactivity. Schools were not meant to be empty. At times like this they seemed lonely and forlorn. Almost sacred, like empty churches.

Ooh, Xander thought. *School . . . sacred . . . Two words that did not belong together.*

He felt like a trespasser. Which, he guessed, they were. He had not asked to come here. In fact, you could say, he came by force. Besides, his dad was the principal. What were they going to do to him? This was one of those times he'd rather not find out.

David asked, "Why the school, do you think?"

"I don't know."

"Do you think it was an accident, or did somebody plan it?"

"I don't know," Xander said again.

"Do you think other people know about it?"

"David, I don't know. I don't know any more than you do. Anything else?"

"Yeah, do you think all the lockers lead somewhere?"

Xander stopped.

David took three more steps before realizing Xander was no longer by his side. He looked back inquisitively.

"One way to find out," Xander said.

David took in the lockers nearest them. "Really?" he said, unsure.

"How else are we going to know?"

"Do we *have* to know?"

Xander thought knowledge was like candy: you never turned it down, especially if you didn't have to work too hard to get it. And especially *cool* knowledge: how to assemble and fire an MI6, how to get your movies to play at Sundance, which lockers were really teleportation devices.

"You don't want to know?" Xander asked.

David thought about it. His face slowly twisted into an I'm-gonna-eat-it-but-I-know-I'm-not-gonna-like-it expression. "Yeah . . . I kinda do."

Xander stepped to the nearest locker, number 76. "You or me?" he asked.

David did not approach. "Um . . . why not both of us?"

"Because in *The Fly*, two life forms teleported at the same time and ended up all mixed together. As much as I love you and all that, I don't want to *be* you."

"I think I saw something like that in *SpongeBob*. It was pretty gross."

"So . . . you or me?"

"You?" David said, closing one eye.

Xander shrugged. He put his foot in the locker.

David stopped him. "No, no, wait. I'll do it. I did it the first time; I can do it again."

Hey, if Dae wanted to. "You sure?"

David climbed in without a word. Xander started to shut the door. David stopped it with his hand. "What if I end up in somebody else's linen closet . . . or worse?"

"What's worse? Like on their dining room table while they're eating? A trash compactor? You want me to go?"

David closed his eyes. "Shut the door."

Xander pushed it until the latch clicked tight.

The scream was hideous. For the first time Xander understood the meaning of the term "bloodcurdling." He pulled up on the latch. His fingers slipped off. The scream went on. He pulled again. Got it. He opened the door. David was hunched over in the tight space.

Laughing.

"Did I get you?" he said.

Xander half-yelled, "You and Dad! What's with you?"

David looked around. "I didn't go anywhere."

"Unfortunately." Xander slammed the door. He stormed toward the double doors at the end of the hall, then pulled up. He turned back to the closed locker door, said, "David, don't keep it up. Don't make me come open that door." The latch rose by itself and the door opened. David popped his head out, displaying a sheepish smile.

Xander said, "You're getting smarter."

David stepped out and approached him.

"Look," Xander said, "all this is weird enough. This is not the time for practical jokes. Don't you think that whatever can take you from home to school faster than a blink could make you scream like you just did?"

David lost his smile. He bowed his head.

"You could have really been in pain, dying," Xander continued. "If we're going to be there for each other, you can't cry wolf. Understand?"

David nodded.

"Next time you scream, it might be for real and I won't come because I think you're joking."

"I know what 'cry wolf' means," David said quietly.

Xander gripped David's shoulder and gave him a little shake. "It's okay. Just don't do it again." When David looked up, Xander saw in his face that he really got it. He didn't want David to be like Dad with his practical jokes, especially now; and he didn't want himself to be like Dad with unending lectures. So he patted David on the back and they walked on.

CHAPTER

eighteen

As they approached the double doors, they heard voices. They looked at each other with wide eyes, looked around for a place to hide. Xander's first thought was the lockers, but David's test didn't prove anything. Any of these lockers could be portals to another place. He looked at David, whose eyes went from the lockers to Xander's face. He had considered the lockers as well and had ruled them out. And they were too far from the nearest classroom to hide in there—*if* the door was even unlocked. He pointed and David moved to the wall beside the door as Xander did the same on the other side. They pressed their bodies against the wall and waited. The voices did not get louder. One of them was Dad's. Xander came off the wall and stepped before a little wire-embedded window set in the door nearest him. Beyond the door was another wide hallway and another set of double doors. Looking down the hallway to his left, he saw his father talking to a man in coveralls. Beside the man was a rolling cart, upon which were a big red toolbox, an assortment of small boxes, and small brown paper bags open at the top. Xander could hear the rhythm of their conversation, but not their words.

Dad was smiling, nodding, probably telling the man about his family, the move here. The man laughed, stooped to reach a lower shelf on his cart, and stood again. He handed Dad what looked like a stack of wooden playing cards. Xander realized they were mousetraps. Dad said something, and the man stooped again for another stack. He turned one of the paper bags over. The clattering sound of dumped nails reached Xander's ears. The man dropped his stack of mousetraps into the bag, then held it open for Dad to do the same. He rolled up the top and handed it to Xander's father. Dad nodded and extended his hand. The man grabbed it and they shook. Dad turned and looked directly at Xander. Xander dropped down below the window, noticing David had been tiptoeing to peer out the window in the other door.

David whispered, "Did he see you?"

"I don't think so." He rose again, expecting to see Dad looming just on the other side. But there he was saying his good-byes and turning to walk in the other direction. Xander caught David's attention and jerked his head to go. They walked quietly away, toward the short corridor at the end of the hallway and locker one-nineteen.

David whispered, "How did they not hear you yelling at me?"

"Or your screams?" Xander thought about it. "Maybe they met out there after all that."

"I hope so. I guess we'll find out when Dad gets home."

"It's not our fault," Xander said, repeating his thoughts from earlier.

"We'll show him what happened. He *can't* blame us."

Xander stopped walking. He looked back at the double doors, saw no sign of anyone. He hunched down to be at David's eye level. "I don't think we should tell Dad," he said. "Or Mom," he added in case that wasn't clear.

"But . . . why not?"

It was a fair question. They were a close family, not in the habit of keeping things from one another. What was embarrassing or personal, dreams and fears—it was all fair game in the King household. Mom had said the world was tough enough without having to worry about hiding things in your own home, from your own family. "So what if you do stupid things?" she'd said. "We're humans, not robots."

Recently, Xander had done some things he had not shared with his family. Just before school finals, a friend had shown him the answer key to the biology exam. Xander hadn't asked how he'd gotten it. But he *had* studied it and aced the test. Another time, Dean had bummed some cigarettes off his older brother, and they'd smoked them behind the school. His dad would have been disappointed, but wouldn't have jumped on him too badly. Still, they were secrets he'd kept from the family. He felt both bad about that and excited to have things they didn't know about. He figured when the time was right, he'd share these experiences and the family's openness would be complete again. Until then, he'd keep these indiscretions in a little footlocker in his mind. The linen closet's fast-track to school would go in there, as well. If his little brother had never needed a footlocker, Xander would have been happy for him. But something told him they were playing with fire. The fewer people burned, the better.

"Something like this will freak them out. They might decide we shouldn't live there. Then we couldn't explore any-more. If the house has a closet like that, what *else* could there be?" He nodded as if to say, *Yeah, this could be fun.*

They went around the corner and David frowned and Xander knew why: his brother didn't like secrets, but neither did he want to move away from the house. At last he said, "Okay, it's just between us. But if it turns bad, we tell them."

Xander stood straight. "Of course."

David stepped into the locker first. Xander shut it and counted to ten. When he opened it again, David was gone.

"I will never get used to this," he said, then stepped into the locker.

Five seconds later, he stepped out of the linen closet into the upstairs hallway, where David was waiting.

CHAPTER

nineteen

Xander and David's late-night conversations had become habit. It helped both of them process the day's events and plan for tomorrow. So this night, like the two before, they faced each other in the motel bed.

"Do you miss Danielle?" David whispered.

"Of course."

"Maybe you'll find a new girlfriend."

"I doubt it. Maybe you will."

David smiled. A year ago, he would have protested that no such thing would *ever* happen, not in a thousand years.

They fell silent. Their parents breathed. Something ticked, ticked.

"I don't think Dad saw us," David said.

"No," Xander agreed. An hour after they had stepped back into the corridor from the closet, from the *school*, Dad had returned home. If he had seen them peering at him from the windows in the doors, he had not let on. He had simply gone about organizing the rest of the upstairs exploration. Both of his sons said they could handle it and had urged him to find something else to do. He had wandered off, moping theatrically. By the time it became too dark to continue, Mom had made short work of the kitchen and butler's pantry—that's what she called the small room with cabinets and counters between the kitchen and dining room. Toria had proclaimed her room ready for furniture and decorations. Dad had walked the grounds, finding nothing of particular interest. And the boys had finished the second-floor investigation. They were all so wiped out, Toria had suggested turning off the television midway through *America's Funniest Home Videos*. Despite its ranking as their favorite show, everyone had agreed.

But now, an hour later, the brothers were wide-awake, sharing their thoughts.

David whispered, "Do you think the closet's the only place that moves you from one place to another?"

"One place like that in the *whole world* is enough," Xander said. Then he thought about how his father had seemed to instantly shift from the dining room to another part of the house when they had first been here. "I think there might be other spots like that in the house. We just haven't found them."

"Yet," David added.

"I was thinking. What if the spots come and go? I saw that in a movie. These portals moved around. Once it was in a phone booth. Another time, in the bathroom of a Chinese restaurant. Same portal, moving around."

"That would suck."

"Yeah. What if you were taking a shower and suddenly you were standing in the middle of a football field at halftime?"

"*Naked?*"

"Shhh." Xander nodded. He could tell David was thinking about it.

"Ooh. That would *really* suck," his brother decided.

"I don't think that could happen."

"Why not?"

"With the closet and the locker, you know what to do to make it work: you step in and shut the door. In the middle of a field, what would you do to return?"

David made a sour face. "Maybe you don't."

"Well, that tells you something, doesn't it?"

"Like what?"

"Like we don't know anything about what we're dealing with. It could be dangerous."

"So . . . should we tell Mom and Dad?"

Toria popped up from the side of the bed nearest David. "Tell them what?"

Both boys screamed in whispers.

"Toria, go back to bed," Xander said.

"Tell Mom and Dad what?"

"That David feels like throwing up."

"Ugh!" She was back in the rollaway before Xander realized she was gone.

"And no," Xander said, almost touching David's nose with his finger. "Don't tell them. Not yet."

David didn't respond for a minute. Then he said, "You know how when we got back from the school, we checked the rest of the second floor and closed closet doors with one of us in it? Shouldn't we go back and do that in the rest of the house?"

"I guess."

"The basement?"

"Everywhere." Xander knew what David was thinking: they'd both been surprised when nothing turned up down there. Now they were going to give it another chance. He thought of all the rooms down there, all the doors. Lots of places to hide a portal. And if there was any correlation between the connected places—the relative brightness and friendliness of a linen closest and a school—where might a portal in the dark, creepy basement lead?

He whispered, "We need to stick together." David said nothing. His eyes were closed. "David?"

A slight snore.

"'Night, Dae," Xander said, and rolled over.

CHAPTER

twenty

The power came on with a *pop! pop! pop!* Xander was standing at the top of the stairs on the second-floor landing when an electric light flared out from the big entryway chandelier. Then three bulbs exploded, one after the other.

"They're on!" he called.

Several lamps in the upstairs corridor came to life as well. One of them blazed bright and went out. The master bedroom suite was down the hall on the opposite side of the house from the kids' bedrooms. Dad hurried out of there now, his eyes surveying the corridor's ceiling lamps.

Down the hall in the other direction, David came out of their bedroom. "Lights on here too!" he said.

Dad said, "I see."

Xander pointed. "Some lights just blew on the chandelier."

Dad nodded as he descended the stairs, two at a time. "Old wiring, plus water and rodent damage, dirt in the sockets . . . I'm gonna throw the breakers until we know it's safe."

"Awww," David moaned.

"Won't be long," Dad said. He disappeared into the corridor under the boys, heading for the kitchen and the basement stairs.

Smoke coiled up from the blown bulbs in the chandelier. "Cool," David said.

Xander elbowed him. "That's *not* cool." He headed toward their bedroom with a bucket of sudsy water. Dad had said their furniture was arriving in the afternoon, and if they wanted to set up their room, it had to be clean first.

David followed him into the bedroom. They had positioned their flashlights on the floor and dresser to illuminate the areas they were cleaning. David had apparently dropped the broom when the lights came on. He picked it up now and began sweeping a pile of dust toward the door. Xander sat the bucket down by one of the windows. He pulled a washcloth out of the water and lathered up the glass. The windows and frames were so filthy, glass cleaner and paper towels simply didn't cut it.

David said, "When are we going to look for more portals?"

"When we get a chance, I guess."

David swept a big cloud into the hallway. Granules of dirt and other debris rained into the hardwood floor and linen closet door on the other side of the hall. He turned around, leaned on the broom handle, and said, "I thought we were going to do it today."

Xander continued to inscribe big, soapy circles on the window. He said, "You want a bedroom, don't you?"

"Yeah, but . . ."

Xander had to smile. "You thought putting your new room together would be the most excitement you'd have after we got here."

"Guess I was wrong." He looked back through the door, at the linen closet.

Xander said, "Don't even think of going in there on your own."

"I'm not."

Xander didn't like the way he said it.

Their bedroom faced the front of the house. As Xander wiped away the soap, he saw a big moving van pull up to the end of the road.

•••••• ••

Until now, Xander had lived in the same house, in the same room, his entire life. That room had been too small to be creative with the placement of the furniture. The most they could do was swap the position of their bunk beds and dresser, change the posters on the walls, and alternate who got to sleep on top.

The bedroom in their new house was huge. Xander had no idea how much fun simply arranging furniture could be. Using bunk beds to save floor space was no longer necessary, and the boys quickly decided to have their own beds with no one above or below them. Each boy had wanted to put his bed in the tower. When the argument got loud, Dad had ruled that neither of them could use it. So the tower became their homework and reading area, with a writing desk and beanbag chair. They had voted to keep the dresser that was already in the room, as well as their old one from Pasadena. That way, each boy would have his own dresser for the first time in their lives.

"I don't know what to do with all the space," David said with a big grin. He was looking into one of the empty drawers of their old dresser, which a losing toss of a coin had awarded him. Neither dresser mattered to Xander, but after he ended up with the one from their new house, he wondered if his things would disappear from any of the drawers. He imagined a pile of boxers suddenly appearing on some family's kitchen counter one day.

Each boy would also get his own night table and bedside lamp. It was almost like having your own room. But not.

Dad's music pounded from the master bedroom. Most of the lyrics and high notes didn't make it as far as the brothers' bedroom, but the bass thumped in the floors and off the walls.

Xander opened a box full of rolled posters and began sorting through them. He selected one and flattened it against the wall above his bed. The edges were torn, the tips of the corners lost long ago. It was a lithograph of a tiled mosaic hanging in Naples' Museo Archeologico Nazionale that featured a scene of Alexander the Great at the Battle of Issus. Xander was named after the ancient Greek king of Macedon.

It was a family tradition, dating as far back as anyone could remember, to name King children after great kings and queens. Fortunately, the practice did not extend to marrying people with royal names. That would really crimp their pursuits of love. Still, Mom insisted there was a Queen Gertrude. Dad said only in Shakespeare's *Hamlet*, and that didn't count.

The Alexander in the poster had long sideburns, down to his jawline—the guy would have been hip today, twenty-three hundred years after his death. Xander touched his own face. He could not grow sideburns yet, just a bit of fuzz; as soon as he could, he would.

"Whatcha think?" he asked David, who had settled on the floor with his PSP. He glanced up at the poster.

"Aren't you sick of looking at that? I am."

Xander let the poster spin back into a roll. He said, "Just because you don't put up the one Mom and Dad gave *you*."

"Michelangelo's *David*? The guy's *naked*."

"It's art."

David made a disgusting sound with his lips. "I'll find a different poster of King David, thank you."

Footsteps in the hallway drew their attention. The clomping boots of the moving men. When they'd arrived, all they wanted to do was grumble about having to haul the stuff through the woods to the house. Then Dad had slipped each of them some extra cash and that was that.

"This one?" someone said.

Another answered, "No, down there. She said by the bedroom." A man came into view carrying a box. He opened the linen closet door and stepped in to slide the box onto one of the shelves. Another mover, coming up behind, bumped the door and it swung shut.

David gasped.

The door didn't latch, however, and the second man kicked it open with his boot. The first man turned in the closet and took the box from his colleague. The second man looked in at them. "Hey, boys."

Xander and David were too stunned to answer. The man gave them a puzzled look, then both movers pushed the closet door shut and clomped away. David turned from the open dresser drawer to stare open-mouthed at Xander, who returned the expression.

David said, "He almost . . ."

Xander nodded. "And another thing . . ." He walked to the linen closet door. David moved up behind him. Xander opened it. Two boxes inside. "It must only work with people."

"Good thing. We'd lose all our towels."

"We'd get them back dirty," Xander said, "along with some kid's schoolbooks."

When they shut the door, they jumped. Dad was standing there. He had turned down the music and they hadn't noticed.

"How you guys doin'?" Dad said.

"Good, good," Xander said, a little too quickly.

"Fine," David said in that higher Toria voice he got when he was scared or nervous.

Dad looked past them into their room. "Getting settled in there?"

"Getting there," Xander said, and went into the bedroom. David and Dad followed. Xander sat on his bare mattress. David sat on his, facing Xander.

"What do you think?" Dad said. "Is this going to work?"

Xander looked around the room appreciatively. "It's cool."

"Yeah," David agreed.

"So . . ." Dad looked from son to son. "Stay here tonight?"

"Really?" David said, hopping up.

Dad said, "If we can get the lights back on." He looked at his watch. "An electrician should be by anytime now."

"All right!" David said.

Xander smiled his agreement. Dad scanned the floor near the walls. "You haven't seen any mice up here, have you?"

Xander shook his head. "Did you catch some?"

"A couple in the kitchen cabinets." He put his finger to his lips in a hushing gesture. "Don't tell your mother."

"Can I see?" David asked.

"Next time."

David furled his brow. "Do they have a mouse problem at the school?"

Xander kicked his leg, then stood to make it look like an accident.

"I don't know," Dad said. "Why?"

Before David could complete the task of wedging his foot into his mouth, Xander said, "I was telling him that rodents are everywhere out here in Hicksville. Not just in old houses."

"Yep," Dad agreed. "They're everywhere." He turned to leave then stopped at the door. "Mom's got the boxes of sheets and blankets in our room. Come get some."

"Be right there," Xander told him.

When he was gone, Xander punched David in the arm. "Idiot."

David frowned. "I'm not used to secrets."

"Everybody has secrets," Xander said, irritated. He brushed past David on his way out the door. Over his shoulder, he said, "Even this house."

•••••••••

Mom was sitting on her bed when Xander looked in. She was examining the pages of a photo album that was open beside her. With her hair falling over her face, he thought at first she was crying. He rapped gently on the master bedroom door. He was relieved to see a beaming smile when she looked up.

"Hey, Xander. Come sit." She patted a clean spot on the bed. Boxes and items wrapped in newspaper covered the rest.

"I came for our sheets and blankets," he said. "Dad said you had a box."

"Oh, sit with your mom a sec, will ya?"

On the way over, he glanced around. "Big," he said.

"Needs some work." She was talking about the old wallpaper, stained and hopelessly outdated. "I like it, though."

When he sat, she tapped a picture in the album. "Remember this?"

Xander about six years old, standing next to Mickey Mouse in front of Sleeping Beauty's Castle at Disneyland. Xander's face was twisted in terror, his face glistening with tears. His mouth was open so wide, you could almost see that little hanging thing at the back of his throat. *Uvula*, he thought it was called. What made it worse was David—three years old, big happy grin, holding Mickey's white-gloved hand.

Xander frowned. "You made me stand next to him. I thought he was creepy." He thought about it. "David was too young to know better, that's all."

She smiled, closed the book. She touched his hand. "I want to show you something." She stood and went to a bookcase, where a half-dozen ceramic figurines had been unwrapped and were on display. She selected one and returned to the bed. She rotated it in her hands. It was a chipped and faded ceramic rooster, about a foot high. He knew it meant a lot to her.

"Nana gave you that before she died," he said. Cancer had taken his grandmother when Xander was two. He sometimes thought he remembered her face, but couldn't be sure.

Mom nodded. "And *her* mother gave it to her. She brought it over from Portugal, when she immigrated to the States. She used to say it was the only thing they had left from the old country, except our blood." She pushed her fingers into a hole in the base of the rooster and pulled something out. It was a fat roll of dollar bills. The outside one was a twenty.

"Mom!" he said in a hoarse whisper.

She held up the roll. She said, "It was going to be a surprise, but this move has been so hard on you . . . It's for your car."

"My *car?*"

"It's not that much yet, and you have to chip in, but maybe by the time you're sixteen . . ."

"But how . . . ?"

"You know we don't have a lot of extra money. When you were born, your father and I decided I'd quit my job and be a full-time mom. That made things tight, but . . ." Her eyes scanned his face. "It was the right decision. Last year, when you started talking about a car, I realized we weren't ready for something like that. The car, gas, insurance . . ." She shook her head. "I started putting a little aside every month. I cut more coupons, didn't go to the hair salon so much."

"Mom . . ." He didn't know what else to say.

"It added up," she said, looking at the wad. She seemed as amazed by its size as Xander was.

"How much is it?" A pang of guilt rippled through him for asking.

"Almost two thousand, but I hope we'll have more by the time you turn sixteen in January."

"Two *grand?*" He leaned over the album and threw his arms around her neck. "Thank you."

"Now, Xander, you have to contribute. I only meant to—"

"I will! I will! I'll get a job as soon as I can!"

"Your bedding is right there. David's too." She indicated a box on the bed.

Unable to stifle his grin, he stood and picked it up. "Thank you," he whispered again.

CHAPTER

twenty-one

SATURDAY, 12:02 A.M.

The bulbs in the bathroom emitted only a dim, yellowish glow. *Better than nothing*, Xander thought, standing in front of the toilet bowl in only his boxers. The electrician had kept the power off in some parts of the house—the basement, the library, the far hallway on the second floor. He'd explained that some wiring and fixtures needed replacing first.

He flushed. The toilet shook and rattled like an excited dog at the end of a short leash. The water in the bowl disappeared in a loud *whoosh*. It filled again with a choking-gurgling sound that made Xander believe stepping into the woods to relieve himself would prove a better experience. At the sink, he turned on the faucet. Water did not immediately come out. Rather, the faucet sputtered and spat. A trickle of water followed, slowly building to a steady flow. He splashed it onto his face and looked at himself in the murky mirror. His hair was a mess, but he didn't look as tired as he felt.

He had tried to sleep, but found himself watching the shadows of branches and leaves play across his ceiling in the moonlight. Finally, he'd tossed his bedding aside and gotten up. His clock had read 11:57. He was glad his mother had put a night-light in the hall; he might have never found the bathroom without it.

He dried his face on a hand towel, relishing its familiarity. Living out of a motel room wasn't the worst thing in the world, but it wasn't home. Neither was their new house yet. Still, as their things from Pasadena started to settle into their new locations, Xander realized these things, as much as his family, would help change that.

When Xander opened the bathroom door, David was there, clad only in pajama bottoms. "Couldn't sleep," he said.

"It's a new place," Xander said. "That's—"

Something fell over in the corridor. The boys spun toward the noise. Boxes were stacked at intervals all the way past the landing to their parents' bedroom. Another night-light glowed at the far end, making the boxes black and their square edges sharply defined. Dad had made a point of telling his kids and the movers to place the boxes against only one wall. That would keep half the hallway open to walk. Now, a box lay in that path just beyond the landing.

"Xander?" David whispered. He stepped back into his brother.

Xander whispered, "Just a box. Someone didn't stack it right."

Another sound reached them. A scraping that seemed to come from the entryway.

David pushed back even farther into Xander.

"Get off my foot," Xander whispered. David didn't budge. "Maybe it's Dad."

"In the dark?" David said.

Xander thought about the way sounds couldn't be trusted in the house. Whatever had made the noise could be anywhere. That made him spin around to look the other direction, toward their bedroom.

David jumped, said, "What?" He grabbed Xander's hand.

"Nothing. Just looking."

A door thunked shut. Somewhere on the first floor . . . maybe. Xander took a step toward their bedroom. "Wait here," he said. He tried to shake him loose, but David was having none of that.

"No way," David said.

"Then you go. The flashlights are on my dresser."

"No way," he repeated. "Turn on the hall light."

"I don't know where the switch is."

"All right," David said. "Stay here." David released his hand and walked to the bedroom. He looked back every second step. He could have been swimming, turning his head regularly to breathe. He hesitated outside the bedroom, then reached his hand around the frame to flip on the light. Moments later, Xander saw the two flashlights come on and shine against the linen closet door.

When David emerged, Xander asked, "Is the switch down there?"

The beams flashed around.

"I don't see it," David said. He hurried to Xander and handed him one of the lights. They moved down the hall toward the landing. Toria's door was open. A night-light revealed her sleeping in bed. David cast his light into the room.

Xander pushed his hand down. "Don't wake her," he whispered. At the landing, they leaned on the banister. Xander panned his light over the base of the stairs, the few feet of dining room visible to him, and the front door.

David shined his light directly below, onto the corridor leading to the kitchen. "It's like we're in a guard tower."

"Shhh." Xander's beam caught the chandelier. A thousand sparkles of white and blue light danced on the walls.

"Whoa," David said. He added his light to Xander's. A galaxy of stars exploded around them, swirling over the walls and their faces. Despite their unease, they shared a smile.

Then David's light fell from his hand. It tumbled end over end, until it crashed on the floor way below and blinked out.

"Dae—" Xander said and stopped. His brother stared wildly at something past Xander. David reached out. He found the flesh of Xander's arm and squeezed.

Xander hissed in pain. He looked over his shoulder, down the hall. Where the corridor made a ninety-degree turn toward the back of the house, a figure stood. Just like the boxes, it was backlit by the night-light. He could make out no features. Who-ever—*whatever*—it was, it appeared huge, but that could have been a trick of the light. "Dad?" he said.

The figure swayed, seeming to shift its weight from one foot to the other. Its arms became more distinct. Muscular and massive.

"That's not Dad," David whispered.

Xander turned to swing his flashlight around. At the same time, David grabbed for it. It flipped out of Xander's hand. He fumbled for it, caught it, and flashed its beam down the hall. The light captured a flash of shoulder, a foot as the person disappeared beyond the corridor's bend. David's other hand shot out, and he sank both sets of fingers into Xander's bare torso.

"What was that?" David said.

"Come on," Xander said. He moved toward the spot where the figure had disappeared.

"No, wait . . . Xander!" David was right on his heels.

"Don't you want to know?" Xander whispered.

"Not like this! Let's wake Dad. Xander! Wait!"

They were approaching their parents' bedroom on the left. It was a wonder Dad wasn't already bolting out to investigate. He suspected the noise had rippled away from their sleeping parents. Whether the house had randomly kept Mom and Dad from hearing the sounds or had done it purposely, Xander could not guess. He hoped it was not intentional.

In any event, he had the opportunity now to burst in and get their help. He pulled up beside their door. The shaking flashlight beam betrayed his nerves. He braced himself, turned to David.

"We have to look ourselves, first," he whispered. "We're right behind him. It may be our only chance to figure out what's going on."

"What's going on is somebody broke into our house."

"How'd he get in? Where was he when we searched?" He tried another tactic: "Look, if it's a false alarm, Dad's going to really think I'm crazy."

"False alarm?" David said between clenched teeth. "Didn't you *see* him?"

"That doesn't mean he's there now."

David knew as well as Xander did that the bend in the hall led only to the servants' quarters. David said, "Where could he have gone?"

"The house, Dae. It doesn't make sense."

"Then what are we doing *living* in it?" He kept looking

past Xander to the bend, so Xander didn't have to.

Xander held his index finger to his mouth. "Shhh," he whispered. "Hear that?"

Somewhere outside, a dog was howling.

For some reason, that bothered Xander even more than seeing an intruder. He said, "Okay, listen. If we're attacked, we go crashing into Mom and Dad's room, sound good? Let's just take a look, see what we see. *Just a look.*"

David reached past a box and picked up a shower curtain rod. He got a two-handed grip on it, shook it to test its weight and balance. "Let's do it," he said.

CHAPTER

twenty-two

Xander and David followed the flashlight beam around the corner. It found the closed guestroom door, and Xander held it there.

"Was it closed before?" he asked.

"I don't know."

Being closed was worse. It meant opening it to who knew what. Stepping nearer, he expected the door to spring open and the man with the big feet to charge out. The backsplash of light filled the hallway. Their own shadows danced around them. David was near enough for Xander to feel his breath on his back. He glanced back at his brother. Big eyes. Tight lips. He held the shower curtain rod straight up, ready to bring it down hard on any head he didn't recognize.

Xander reached for the door handle. He turned it slowly, listening to the metal inside grinding against itself. The latch disengaged from the receptacle in the frame. He pushed. A musty odor drifted out. He pointed the flashlight at the black breach. It illuminated a thin strip of hardwood floor, a slice of furniture deeper inside. He debated kicking at the door, then decided to simply push it fully open. Extending his arm, he hoped nothing reached through and grabbed him.

David tapped his shoulder. Xander did not want to turn his attention from the partially open door. "What is it?" he whispered.

"Look."

"Now?"

Instead of answering, David tapped him again.

Xander looked, saw him nod to his other side. Xander swiveled his head around that way. On the back wall, where the hall ended, a thick shadow, straight as a ruler, ran from floor to ceiling. He turned the flashlight's beam to it. Part of the wall was canted out, open like a door that had not closed fully. The wall had been paneled in vertical planks of wood.

The opening matched where two planks met, which explained why they had not spotted the secret door before.

Xander pulled the guest room door closed. He no longer thought anyone occupied the room, but he didn't want to make it easy for someone to sneak up on them if he was wrong. He tiptoed to the movable wall. Before he could get his fingers to the edge, David reached out and pushed it shut. It clicked and remained flush with the rest of the wall.

"Dae!" he whispered. "What if we can't get it open again? We don't know where the—"

David gave the wall a quick push and it popped open a crack.

Xander scowled at him. "Good thing." He pulled at the edge. It swung toward them easily, silently. He reversed a step, bumping into David and pushing him backward. The flashlight picked up another wall several yards beyond the fake one. He moved into the opening. A closed door was set in the second wall. A sheet of metal had been riveted to it, as if to strengthen it. Xander approached it, feeling David clinging to him like a wet leaf.

"Check it out," he said quietly.

Hanging from a bright metal hasp, attached to the door, was a heavy padlock. Dangling with the lock was the portion of the hasp that had been screwed to the door frame. It had been ripped out, broken when the door was forced open. Splinters of wood lay at the baseboard, a screw not far away.

"It looks new," David said.

Xander turned the handle and pulled the door open. Stairs ascended to the floor above. But he and David had already found the attic entrance on the other side of the house. He recalled how small the attic had been, how he had assumed it was because of the shape of the roof. Now he thought of another reason: there were *two* attics.

He didn't like it. This was right out of a *Goosebumps* story: snoopy visitors would find the stairs to the attic, go up, and . . . well, what happened to them wasn't pretty.

Xander's light revealed nothing at the top of the flight. The landing was deep enough to mask any door or wall that might be at the top.

David was peering around Xander, pressing his chest against Xander's back. Xander could feel the boy's racing heart, and more: he was shivering as violently as a person who'd fallen through a lake's frozen surface. Xander stepped back and closed the metal-skinned door.

He took in his brother's frightened face, wondered how much of it mirrored his own expression. He had read somewhere that bravery is not the absence of fear but the forging ahead despite being afraid. David was certainly afraid, but he'd seen his brother's bravery too many times to assume he wanted to end their adventure here and now.

"You okay?" he asked.

David nodded and actually bent his lips into a smile of sorts.

"Your call. We go up now . . . or wait till tomorrow, get Dad's help if you want."

David stared at the door, considering his options. His heartbeat continued to pound furiously against Xander's back.

At length, he whispered, "What I said before: let's do it."

Xander felt himself shiver. It was more internal than David's vibrating goose bumps, but a sign of his fear, all the same. Maybe he had been counting on David to vote them off this island, to send them home, back to bed. Perhaps his brother's fear was contagious. *Bravery isn't the absence of fear*, he reminded himself. He just wished he had something like David's curtain rod to wield. A bat would be nice. So would an M16. And he didn't much like the idea that he was almost naked, except for boxers. Going into battle required a uniform, didn't it? At least *clothes*. Did he say *battle*? Not battle. No, not battle. Just . . . just . . . checking out a new place in their home. That's all.

Yeah, a new place behind a fake wall and a door with a broken lock, where some huge dude is probably waiting to ambush you.

Stop it, he scolded himself. *Are you going to do this or not?*

David, right behind him, had said, "Let's do it." How could Xander back out now? He'd never live it down.

He pulled open the door again, flashed the light up the stairs. Nothing lurked at the top . . . that he could see. He passed through the threshold, then mounted the first step. The second. The third.

David stayed one step below him.

Another step. A wall came into view, just past the upper landing.

Up to step number . . . he'd forgotten. Didn't matter. David kept a hand on Xander's hip. He was so close, Xander felt he was giving his brother a piggyback ride.

He stepped onto the landing. Set at a ninety-degree angle from the stairway was a long, dark corridor.

David edged up behind him. He said, "Xander, look."

On the left wall was an old-fashioned light switch: a copper faceplate through which two push-buttons, one over the other, protruded. The upper button was depressed, almost flush with the faceplate. The bottom button stuck out a half inch farther. Xander pushed this one, which caused the top button to pop out, teeter-totter style. The corridor lit up, illuminated by lights in the ceiling as well as wall-mounted lamps, spaced at even intervals on both long walls. The hallway wasn't straight; it bent slightly this way then that way, like a snake. It never curved enough to block the far end from view. And its length puzzled Xander. It seemed longer than the house itself, which was impossible. He wondered if the wall on the far end was mirrored, giving the hallway its extended appearance. The floor was hardwood, as was the rest of the house, but an old-fashioned carpet, red with an intricate black pattern, ran the length of the corridor. The bottom third of the walls was wainscoted in squares of dark wood. Wallpaper covered the upper portion: vertical stripes of old vines and leaves over an ivory background. Doors lined both sides. They were staggered so no one door faced another. Their handles glinted dully in the light.

"Holy cow," David whispered. "What is it?"

"I don't know."

"It looks like a hotel," David said.

"A hotel designed by Dr. Seuss, maybe," Xander added.

"Do you think the guy we saw is in one of these rooms?"

The *figure*. Xander's nerves were coiled on the razor edge between fight and flight. The figure had become symbolic of anything this house could throw at him. But David had kept the threat focused. It was not a row of doors that could harm them. It was what could come out of those doors.

"Well . . ." Xander answered, taking a tentative step into the hallway, "there's only one way to find out."

twenty-three

SATURDAY, 12:27 A.M.

The curvy corridor lay before them. It was creepy and mysterious and oddly inviting.

Both boys had stepped onto the carpeted runner. It was soft and warm under Xander's bare feet. He forced himself to start walking. David clung to him like one of those remora fish that attached themselves to sharks. It made Xander feel like the big brother he was. When it came to tackling new adventures, David was fearless. As long as he knew others had trod before him and lived, he figured he could do it too. What spooked the kid was . . . well, *spooky* things: ghosts, vampires, dark shadows, mysterious noises. The unknown.

My turn to be brave, Xander thought.

They approached the first light fixture. It was a small statue mounted to the wall: an old man, whose long beard flowed into a tunic. A wreath crowned his head. He held open a book and pointed at a page. His eyes were cut out, allowing the light from the bulb within to shine through them. Xander recognized the style of the carving as ancient Greek—one of the things about having a history teacher for a dad was you got a lot of history lessons. He suspected the man was Plato or Socrates or one of the other brainy sage-types. The top of the lamp was open. Light splashed up the wall in the shape of an ice-cream cone. The ice-cream scoop itself was a glowing circle on the ceiling. As they passed, Xander's eyes kept darting back to the decorative fixture. He half-expected the old man to turn his head, following their progress.

David jabbed him in the ribs.

"Ow, what?" Xander said. David was pointing. The wallpaper had been peeled away in four thin, horizontal furrows. The rips were as long as Xander's arm. One ended in a bunched-up wad of wallpaper; at the end of the other three furrows, rippled strips of paper hung like the tails of rats.

"Claw marks," David whispered.

"Maybe," Xander said, but that's exactly what they looked like.

They were a few feet from the first door. It was six-paneled and stained dark brown, like the others in the house. On the front of the door handle was a face: a scowling man whose tight lips appeared ready to open for a hearty reprimand. A brass plate under the handle was etched in the same intricate pattern as the carpeted runner. The impression of an old hotel was so strong in his mind, Xander was mildly surprised that no room number was affixed to the door.

"What do we do?" David whispered behind him.

"I'm thinking." He had a mind to knock—another remnant of the hotel milieu. Or maybe he thought politeness would spare him the wrath of whoever might be lurking on the other side. Instead, he turned the knob and pushed open the door. A small room lay within. A single domed fixture in the ceiling cast the room in a harsh, bright light. Xander pushed the door farther until it stopped against the left-hand wall. He could see through the crack between door and frame, on the hinged side, that no one was waiting to jump out.

Xander stepped in.

David hung back, putting more than a hair's distance between them for the first time since they saw the figure downstairs. He looked up the hall in both directions, apparently decided that being in the strange room with Xander was better than being outside it without him, and stepped in.

147

A wooden bench ran the length of the wall on the right. A shelf with a series of heavy brass coat hooks below it was above the bench, slightly higher than Xander's eye level. Hanging on the hooks were the accoutrements of a day at the beach: a man's bathing suit, a colorful beach towel, swimming fins, snorkel, and mask. A beach umbrella, extending from bench to ceiling, leaned into a corner. Next to the umbrella, two blue and white flip-flops sat side by side. Opposite the entrance was another door. It felt like they were in a mudroom.

Xander stepped to the inner door. Slowly, he gripped the handle. "It's locked," he informed David.

"From the other side?"

Xander looked at the handle. There was no keyhole. No deadbolt or any other hardware on the door. Even the hinges must have been on the other side, for they were invisible to him. He tried the handle again. It was as solid as a dock's mooring cleat. If it could be unlocked only from the other side, then it must also be locked from that side. The implications hit Xander like a plank upside his head. He pressed his palms against the door, holding it shut. He swung his face around to David.

"It's locked from the other side," he said, almost hissing out the words. "You can't unlock it from this side. That means—"

"There's somebody in there!" David finished.

"Can you see anything under the door?"

David dropped. He pressed his cheek against the wood floor. "Nothing. It's all black."

Xander kept leaning into the door, sure something was about to push through. He tilted his head to put an ear against the surface. Something on the other side scraped the door. He said, "Get out! Go! Now!"

David scrambled up. He backed through the open door into the hall.

"Xander?" he said, sounding like he was ready to cry.

Xander came off the door. He backpedaled out of the room, pulling the first door shut as he did.

His grip remained tight on the handle. At last, he let go and backed away. He and David stared at the door a long time.

"What'd you hear?" David said.

Scraping.

"Think it was *him*?"

"Has to be."

David scanned the other doors down the hall. "You want to check the other doors?"

"Why?" Xander said.

"If he's in *this* one, he's not in those. Maybe we'll find something to help us."

David was the video game player of the family. He tended to think this way: strategically. When Xander got stuck on *Halo 3*, David jumped in and methodically checked each possibility until he found the answer.

Xander doubted snapping a beach towel at the figure would do any good. But tools or weapons, now that was another story.

At the very least, they might be able to determine the size of the locked room by examining the other rooms. He wasn't sure exactly how that information would assist them, but didn't the hero in every movie, from war spectacles to horror flicks, gather intelligence about his opponent? Often, the solution lay in outwitting the bad guys, not overpowering them.

"Good idea," he said. He stepped past David to the next door. It was on the other side of the hall from the first. Before he could open it, David stopped him.

He gestured toward the first room they had looked into. "What if he comes out of *there*, while we're in *here*?"

Xander didn't have an answer. "You want to go back downstairs?" he said. "Go to bed?"

David shook his head.

Xander opened the door into a room precisely like the first: the bench, the shelf, the second door set in the opposing wall. The only difference were the items left behind. There was a white parka with a fur-lined hood, goggles, binoculars, a white canvas bag adorned by a fat red plus sign. Propped into the corner was a pair of beat-up skis. Beside them on the bench were what appeared to Xander's untrained eye to be two sticks of dynamite. Long fuses. Wrapped in thin red paper, stains showing through. *Nitroglycerin*, Xander thought.

"Are those real?" David asked.

"Don't touch them."

"What's with all this stuff?" David said.

Xander shook his head. "It's like a closet for storing a few things you'd need for one activity. The beach stuff in the other room, the . . . I guess *alpine* things here."

"*Dynamite?*"

Xander shrugged.

"Why?"

"David, I'm seeing this for the first time, like you."

"Check the door."

The second door was locked, as the one in the other room had been. He tried to force the doorknob to turn. Clockwise, counterclockwise—it wouldn't budge. His body rocked as he attempted to rattle the door. It didn't move or make a sound. "How . . . it's *impossible*," he said.

"There's not somebody in that room, too, is there?"

"I hope not." He put his ear against it. He pulled back fast, almost ran, but didn't. "It's the same sound," he whispered.

"Fingernails?" David was moving toward the corridor.

Xander listened again. "More like *wind*. Something blowing around in the wind. Sand, maybe. Leaves and twigs."

"Does it lead outside?"

"Can't," Xander said. "I've inspected the outside of the house. There are some dormer windows in the attic. Nothing like this, no doors."

"Is it a *real* door?" David said.

Xander stared at him, thinking. "Like . . . maybe it's not a door at all." As David had done earlier, Xander got onto the floor to look under the door. "It doesn't look like it just stops there." Remaining on his knees, he looked around. He rose and stepped to the skis. His hand was inches from them when he stopped. What if it was a trap? What if every item was booby trapped somehow? He pulled his hand away. To David he said, "Give me your pajamas."

"They're my *pants*," David protested.

"I'll give them right back."

David tugged at the drawstring, unraveling a bow. He pulled them off. In only boxers now, as Xander was, he hesitated, then handed over his pajama bottoms. The material was thin and lightweight, as Xander had expected. He dropped to his knees again and began pushing one of the pant legs under the door. "Hey!" David said.

"I just want to see if there's space on the other side of the door . . . or if there's a wall. I told you I'd—" The pajamas ripped out of his hands. They zipped under the door and were gone, so fast their final moments were a blur. Xander jumped back. He crashed into David, who had already spun halfway out of the room. Xander grabbed him and shoved him toward the stairwell.

"Go, go, go!" he yelled.

CHAPTER

twenty-four

The brothers tripped and banged into each other as they flew past the first door and the Plato wall light. At the landing, David tromped down. Xander turned to look back. Nothing was after them. "Wait!" he said.

David stopped. "Are they coming?" he asked.

Xander shook his head.

"What was that? What happened to my pajamas?" He was slowly reascending the stairs.

Xander looked at his palms, as if for clues. "They were just pulled out of my hands."

"So somebody *was* in the locked room."

Xander thought about it. Somehow, the way the pajamas vanished didn't feel like someone yanking them away. "There was kind of a breeze when it happened."

"Yeah, anything moving that fast is gonna make its own wind."

"Not like that. I mean right before they disappeared."

"So, what now?"

Xander smiled. "We keep looking." He started down the corridor.

"Well," David said, coming up behind him, "if you want any more clothes, use your boxers." He chuckled at that.

"Funny."

Both of them kept their eyes on each door they passed. The first one, then the second. They reached another wall lamp, this one completely different from the last. It appeared to be half of a large, ornate goblet. Lead or pewter, maybe. There was a flat base; a stem that resembled a vine-entwined column; and a chalice inlaid with colored glass pieces, cut like gems. Light not only poured from its open top, up the wall to the ceiling, but also gleamed through the colored glass. He saw now that each fixture was different, but he could not tell at this distance what each one resembled.

The next room they entered was much like the first two: bench, shelf, locked second door. The theme of the items had something to do with war. There was a smooth, round helmet; binoculars—black, not white as the ones in the Alpine room were; and a gun belt with bullets and a holster, but no gun. On the bench was a hand grenade.

Xander nudged David. "Don't touch *that*, either."

They went from room to room, finding the same arrangement of bench, shelf, hooks, and locked door. The items within reflected a wide range of activities, from mountain climbing to boating to something to do with hunting. Several times Xander and David were at a loss for what the items meant. They reached the end of the long hall and the final door.

"I counted twenty," Xander said.

David nodded. "I lost count at twelve."

Xander noted that the wall at the end of the hallway was not mirrored but decorated to match the side walls. The landing at the other end, where they had started, seemed far away.

To make their investigation complete, they stepped through the last door. Hanging from the hooks were the props from a costume play: a round shield, battered and bent; a simple helmet, equally scarred; a scabbard with a sword's hilt extending from it; a net, made of steel links; and what appeared to be an animal pelt. Xander tried the interior door, knowing what he would find: it was locked. When he turned away, his heart leaped into his throat. David was holding the scabbard, pulling the sword from it.

"David! Don't touch it!"

His face was beaming. "Why not? This is cool!"

Xander grabbed his brother's hands, preventing him from pulling the short sword all the way out. "It might be a trick," he said. He listened for any sounds that might reach him from the hall. No doors clicking open. No footsteps.

David watched him listen without saying a word. They stood like that—both boys in only boxers, sword and scabbard held between them—for a long time. It did not escape Xander how strange it was that he was more worried about the props than about their intrusion into the rooms. Rooms were rooms. A man's tools, his weapons, were part of who he was, part of what he did. To Xander, his camera said more about him than his bedroom. He did not know in what way, but he suspected the items in these rooms were more important than the rooms themselves. Because of that, if there was a trap, he believed the spring, the trigger, would be among them.

With a stillness, a quiet, he began to relax. He released his brother's hands.

David, spooked now, did not move. He said, "What is it?"

Xander smiled. He nodded toward the sword. "Let's see it." It came out of the scabbard with a metallic *shiiing!* David held it up. The blade was two feet long, thick, tapering to a fine point. It was dinged and scratched with rust and—

"Is that blood?" David asked, staring.

"Stage blood," Xander said with more certainty than he felt.

David rotated his wrist, circumscribing a figure eight in the air with the tip.

Xander cautiously plucked the helmet off the hook. He hefted it in his hands. He said, "This thing's heavy." It felt gritty under his fingers, as though it was rusting or had been lying in dirt. He checked inside, then fitted it over his head.

David laughed. "Gluteus Maximus, I salute thee!"

Xander pulled the metal net off its hook. It too was heavy, even heavier than the helmet. About the length of the sword, it was formed into a tube, open at both ends, but wider on one side than the other. Leather straps were attached to the wide end. He understood what it was. He stuck his arm into the tube up to his shoulder. His hand popped out the other end, where a metal band crossed over his palm. He tugged on the straps and cinched the ends together like a belt under his opposite arm.

"Whoa!" David said.

Xander flexed out his chest, held up his arm. "Chain mail," he said. His arm almost immediately felt the strain of the chain's weight. He lowered his hand, resting it on the locked door handle. "I know what all this—" The handle rotated under his palm. He fell to the floor as the door clicked open.

David screamed and dropped the scabbard. He squared himself to the door. He held the sword in both hands, extending his arms before him.

Xander scrambled up. He stood next to David. Light, *sunlight*, streamed through the three-inch opening. Nothing on the other side interrupted the flow of light. No shadows cast by beast or man as they prepared to push through. A sound, not dissimilar to the wind in the trees, reached their ears. Beyond it was a muted rumble, like a distant surf.

"Xander?" David said.

That spurred Xander to move. He approached the door. He cocked his head to see through. Only light. He reached out, touched the edge of the door, and pulled it open.

David sucked in a sharp breath. Beyond the threshold was nothing that could be part of the house. It was a vast landscape of sand. An unfelt wind whipped the grains into spinning dervishes that danced for a few seconds before settling again. New torrents sprang up in different spots. Nearby, rocks broke the surface of the dunes. They huddled low as if avoiding the sting of flying sand.

The heat of a midday sun radiated over the boys. *Impossible,* Xander thought. *It must be about one o'clock in the morning. Here, anyway . . . certainly not in there.* Sand blew in. Xander felt it hit his legs and then his stomach and chest. It was drifting in, obscuring more and more of the hardwood floor. He stepped closer, put his hand on the door frame. He stretched his leg past the threshold.

"Xander, don't!" David yelled.

"I'm just *seeing,*" he said over his shoulder.

He pushed his bare foot into the hot sand. It sank in a half inch. This was no hallucination, though he didn't really think it was, with David seeing it too. Xander released the door frame and took another step. He was completely out of the little room now.

"Xander!" David screamed again.

Xander looked back, grinning at the wonder of it all.

The door slammed shut.

CHAPTER

twenty-five

SATURDAY, 1:11 A.M.

David couldn't believe it.

Oh, no, no, no, no, no . . .

He tossed the sword aside and leaped for the door. Both hands on the handle. It turned. He tugged at it and it opened— six inches, no more. Something seemed to be tugging back, and he lost an inch of opening. Every muscle strained to pull the door open.

"Xander! Xander!"

He raised his foot and pressed it into the wall beside the door.

Pulled . . . pulled.

Quickly, he moved one hand from the knob to the edge of the door, wrapping his fingers around to the other side. Then he moved his other hand. He felt the heat of the sun, the tickling of the sand on his fingers and his ankle.

Where was Xander? Wouldn't he be calling? Wouldn't he push from the other side?

Grunting and straining with everything he had, he lost another inch of opening. Four inches. His knuckles were close to the edge of the doorframe. His hands were white, the blood squeezed out of them. If he eased up now, if he took a breath, the door would slam shut, taking eight of his fingers with it.

The door closed farther.

Noooo!

Now the muscles in his legs, his arms, even his stomach, were burning in pain. The door pulled in farther. His vision blurred as tears filled his eyes. With a scream of anguish, he snapped his fingers out from the narrowing crack. The door slammed with a solid *bang!* Despite his muscles feeling stretched like taffy, he seized the door handle. It would not turn.

"Uh . . . uh . . ." His sounds were cries and calls and groans all at once. He tugged, but the door held firm. He dropped to the floor, held his lips to the gap. "Xander! Can you hear me?"

In the little room, individual grains of sand began rolling across the hardwood floor toward the gap. More and more sand disappeared under the door. Believing it signaled some kind of finality, David slammed his hand down on the sand. He felt it grating against his skin. It slid out and flew out beneath the door.

"No, no." He laid his forearm in front of the gap, wedging it between door and floor. Sand whipped around his elbow and away. It formed a drift against his arm, then sailed over; some pushed under. He lay down in front of the gap. He felt the insistent tug of the wind like a vacuum. His boxers fluttered, trying to follow the sand through the gap. The grains kept flowing past, faster and faster, until he felt and saw no more and the suction coming from the gap stopped. He flipped himself around and held his eye to the base of the door. The light beyond faded and went black.

twenty-six

When Xander first looked back, David was standing in the small room. He was holding the sword out in front of him. Panic made his eyes wide. The streaming sunlight made his skin pale. He mouthed Xander's name—Xander recognized the movements of his mouth, but did not hear the word come out. The wind was howling out here.

Then a funny thing happened to his vision. David—in fact, the entire rectangle of the threshold and everything it framed—*rippled*. It wavered, as though superheated air had passed between Xander and his brother. Then the door slammed shut, silently and instantly. The frame and door rippled again . . . then simply vanished.

He was staring at endless sand. Mountains in the distance. The roaring surf sound grew louder and the mountains rushed in at him. Surprised, he covered his face with his arm and took a step back. He tripped and went down. Peering over his forearm, he witnessed the mountains become something else. First, they elongated into stone cliffs. Then, faster than a heartbeat, they formed into stadium bleachers. In another heartbeat, the bleachers were crowded with people. The roar was theirs: loud cheers, unrestrained enthusiasm.

Reposed on one elbow, he rotated his head. The stadium completely encircled him. The rocks nearest him shimmered and became a body. It was cut and bloodied. The other rocks he had seen from the small room did the same, until more than two dozen corpses were scattered around the sandy stadium floor. The sand itself took on a darker tint, as though a cloud had rolled over the sun. It was darkest around the bodies and severed limbs. Xander knew it was hued not by shadow but by blood.

The top level of the stadium was lined with ornate columns. Above them, wood poles held canvas awnings, which flapped in the wind. He recognized this place. It was the Roman Colosseum. His father had shown him pictures. But the crowd did not sit in the ruins he had seen. The highest level of the oval was unbroken. The surfaces were crisp and polished, throwing back the sun in a hundred places.

When was the Colosseum finished? He tried to remember. The Emperor Titus had ordered the inaugural games in . . . in the year 80. *Not long after Jesus Christ was crucified!*

Xander pushed himself onto his knees.

The tone of the crowd changed. From within the victorious rumble came a gasp of surprise.

Xander stood. He glanced around. Sure enough, the portal was gone.

Guess I was wrong about where you could end up. Not quite a football field, but close.

The crowd closest to him began an angry chant: "*Sine missione! Sine missione!*"

They pointed at him, raised their hands, then pointed again, as if lashing at him with whips. The chanting and whipping of hands was picked up by more and more people, sweeping the stadium in two directions, outward from the section that had started it.

"*Sine missione! Sine missione!*"

Xander followed its progression, as clear to him as the terminator line between night and day was to astronauts. As he rotated, his eyes fell on the only other living man in the arena. His back was turned against Xander. His arms were raised as he received an ovation of stomping feet and raised voices. Flowers and petals rained down before him. One hand held a sword, the other a shield. He started strutting back and forth, pumping his sword and shield into the air. Then he caught the change of the crowd, their shift from joy to anger. He stopped. He scanned the stands on his side of the stadium.

"Sine missione! Sine missione!"

He spun and spotted Xander. He lowered his arms. He tossed back his shoulders—the gladiatorial equivalent of a bull digging his hoof into the ground, Xander decided. The man strode toward him.

He thinks I'm an opponent he missed, Xander realized. And he looked like one: almost naked, wearing a helmet and chain mail. He held out his hands. "Wait!" he yelled. "Hold on! This isn't what you think! I don't belong here!"

The gladiator was thirty yards away. He showed no sign of stopping. He began waving his sword in the air, then clanged it against his shield. The crowd roared.

Xander backed away. He tripped over something. His cheek hit the dirt. A dead man stared at him from two feet away. The top of his head had taken a severe chop. It was cleaved at his eyebrows. Xander screamed unintelligibly. He got to his feet.

The gladiator was fifteen yards from him, moving in fast. He clutched a long-stemmed rose in his teeth. A red petal fell with each of his thunderous steps.

"I said wait!" Xander pleaded.

The man spat out the stem. *"Morere honeste, sceleste!"* he said.

"What? No, wait!"

The gladiator was so close now, Xander could see the oily sweat that covered his body, the enumerable scars, the splattered blood from his victims, the green pulp from the stem dribbling down his chin.

"I'm just a kid!" Xander yelled. He turned and ran all-out to the curving wall of the arena. He found a wooden door the size of a garage entrance and pounded on it. "Help! Help!"

Where's the portal? How do I get back if the portal's not where it dropped me off?

The thrumming of the crowd rose in pitch. Xander spun to see the gladiator charging him, sword raised over his head.

Xander dropped straight down. The man brought the blade down. It thunked into the door. Xander darted out from under him. He felt a sandaled foot strike his thigh. He fell, kept moving, crawling, crawling in the dirt. He got his feet under him again. He did not look back, but stayed low and shot away. His feet lost traction, but he dug in, dug in and ran. He glanced back. He had put some ground between them. The man jogged toward him, a practiced pace that conserved energy.

Xander spotted a canopied area in the stadium. Flags and brightly breastplated soldiers surrounded several people sitting in wide, ornate chairs. One of them must be the emperor or governor or senator—somebody important. He ran for them, waving his arms frantically.

"Please! Please! I don't belong here! Please!"

Whoever the toga-clad man in the VIP section was, he seemed

to take notice, seemed to understand him. He stood suddenly. His white, closely trimmed beard turned into a hairy frown.

"Please!" Xander yelled.

The man turned to a soldier, barked an order.

The soldier stepped forward, raised a spear, and hurled it at Xander.

Xander turned his shoulder away just as it sailed past. He glared at the long shaft of the spear, wobbling from the effort of piercing the ground. Another soldier threw another spear. Xander dodged, and it impaled a body lying in the dirt. He got the message: no talking to the audience.

He darted away before another soldier used him for target practice.

twenty-seven

While Xander had tried to get help from the bonehead who'd had his soldiers attack him, the gladiator had closed the distance between them. When he looked away, the big man made a sharp turn to cut him off. His feet skidded out from under him, and he went down. The crowd let out a loud and sustained "*booooo!*"

Xander didn't wait to see what happened next. He sprinted the length of the arena, skirting bodies and body parts.

Once again, he reached a large wooden door and pounded his fists on it. He wondered how many of the dead men on the ground around him had done the same thing. This wasn't going to work.

He spied the gladiator jogging toward him. He couldn't play keep-away forever. He'd seen the movie: they'd do something to make sure he was caught. Somehow—maybe with chained wild animals or legionnaires with razor-sharp blades—they'd shrink the area of combat until he had no choice but to face the gladiator.

He ran to the nearest body—a boy not much older than Xander. The wounds made Xander fall to his knees and vomit. His panic had kept his stomach from betraying him until now. Once he'd decided to defend himself, his mind became more rational. And any rational person would have puked at the sight.

The crowd cheered with delight.

Xander wiped his mouth on his bare forearm. He spat and crawled over to the dead boy. It seemed that death had not relieved him from the desire to possess a weapon; the boy's hand held firm to the handle of a mace. Xander pried his fingers open, feeling his stomach lurch again at the stiffness of the corpse's joints. He lifted the powerful weapon, which consisted of a stocky handle, a length of chain, and a heavy shot put–like metal ball tricked out with spikes.

He clambered up. His right arm was heavy and slow, weighed

down by the chain mail and mace. He used both hands to lift the weapon. He hefted it and swung it to his left. The ball moved sluggishly, as though Xander were trying to fight underwater.

The gladiator approached.

Xander pulled the handle to his right. The ball swung with it. He had to throw his hips back to avoid being hit by his own mace, but he thought he had figured something out. Once the ball was moving, it didn't want to stop. All Xander had to do was get it going and steer it. He pumped his arms, as though he were stirring a vat of molasses. The ball swung out in front of him. It came back to his left side. When it swung out again, he pulled it toward his right. This kept the ball swinging in a semicircle around him. The problem was, he couldn't get it higher than his stomach. Still, the gladiator seemed intimidated by this display. Perhaps he believed it was a cunning trick to lure an unsuspecting foe near, at which point a fancy flick of the wrist would send the ball skyward and down on the opponent's head.

If only, Xander thought.

The chain, kept taut now, did not make the *chinking*, chainlike sound Xander expected. It was the ball that emanated the sound of danger, with a *whoosh-whoosh* as it cut through the air. At his right ear, the chain mail's metal rings scraped together, reminding Xander of pebbles dropped onto a metal slide. These sounds, and the grunting of the gladiator, occupied Xander's auditory sense. The crowd had ceased to be. Xander was in a zone that maybe his brother would understand on a very minimal level because of his gaming acumen: two combatants . . . life and death . . . nothing else mattered.

Focus would make him better than he was. Still, he was outmatched. The gladiator possessed skill and experience and bloodlust and the strength to turn these things into a killing machine. The way he glared at Xander, Xander realized he was also focused—focused on bringing down this last stubborn opponent.

As the mace reached its leftward apex, Xander heaved up on its handle. The ball arced up. It passed in front of Xander, level with the gladiator's head. This potentially fatal move was impressive . . . and completely unsustainable. As it swung out, it dropped heavily, all the way to the ground. It took Xander with it, yanking him off his feet, like a novice water-skier. He tumbled over it and wound up on his stomach, staring up at the gladiator jogging toward him. The man was laughing.

Xander scrambled to his feet and ran. He had decided to take a stand, but now was no time to learn how to use a new weapon. Especially one as exotic as an ancient mace. To his untrained and underdeveloped arms, it was nothing more than an anchor. If he had tried that last move while the gladiator was moving in for the kill, Xander would be dead now.

He spotted another body at the far end of the arena and turned toward it. The chain mail on his arm was heavier and heavier. Wearing it was like carrying an anchor. As his feet dug into the sand, he unlashed the strap under his arm and let the chain mail fall away. As much protection as it provided, he needed agility more. Besides, it may have prevented a blow from that gladiator's sword from cleaving off his arm, but without doubt, such a blow would shatter his bones. In agony, without the use of his arm, the gladiator's coup de grâce would have come swiftly.

Xander skidded next to the damaged body. A sword lay in the sand beside it. The handle was sticky with blood.

All the better to keep my grip, Xander thought. He stood and faced the gladiator, who had closed the distance faster than Xander had expected. Xander swung the sword in front of him and screamed. What came out was guttural and animalistic and represented exactly what he felt inside.

The gladiator sneered. It was the same twisting of the lips Xander had witnessed on the faces of countless bullies. It dawned on him that the gladiator was a bully to the extreme.

The man lumbered forward.

Despite his resolve, Xander took a step back. Then another. The top of a round boulder protruding from the sand caught his attention. Of course, it couldn't have been a boulder: Just beneath the sand of the coliseum arena was a wood floor. Under that was the hypogeum, tunnels and rooms where the amphitheater managers kept slaves and animals before spitting them out for the entertainment of the crowd. The "boulder" was a shield. He sidestepped over, stooped to pick it up.

The gladiator rushed in.

Something prevented Xander from gripping the strap behind the shield. The gladiator loomed over him, raising his sword. The weapon disappeared in the brightness of the sun. With no time to wield it perfectly, Xander dropped his sword and clutched the perimeter of the shield. He lifted it over him and ducked his head under it. The gladiator's sword slammed into the shield. It felt as though Xander were trying to hold back a battering ram. Metal clanged. The impact rattled his hands and vibrated up his arms to his shoulders. Instant pain.

But nothing like it could have been, he thought. *Nothing like the sting of death.*

With the shield pushed down onto him, he saw the reason he could not wield it properly. Another arm was already in the shield's straps. It had been severed mid-bicep, at the edge of the shield. The dead fingers waggled at Xander, as if bidding him farewell.

CHAPTER

twenty-eight

Again, the sword came down on the shield, bending it in at the center. He hoped the gladiator would not notice his fingers and lop them off. The sword struck again. A central blow that drove Xander backward, onto his butt. His legs were unprotected now, and one more blow would pitch him onto his back. The tip of the sword scraped the shield as the man lifted it out of the crease he had made.

Xander released one hand from the shield. He put all

his strength into swinging it around, aiming at the gladiator's knees.

The gladiator was no fool.

Obviously accustomed to last-ditch efforts at survival, he reeled back. The shield missed its mark. Xander lost his grip and it sailed away.

Even before the gladiator had started moving away from it, Xander had grabbed his sword and slipped a foot under himself. By the time the shield left his hand, he was already leaping forward. The tip of the blade trailed the shield's trajectory by no more than a second. It was extended farther than the shield, thanks to Xander's forward momentum. It clipped the gladiator's left shin and then his right. Little bleeding mouths opened up under both knees.

The man howled and staggered back. He did not fall. He bowed to examine his wounds. *Probably*, Xander thought, *if the man lost a leg, he would pick it up and beat his opponent with it.*

Xander saw his strike had caused little damage. He pushed himself up and again ran. There was no shame in it. He was there to survive, not honor Caesar or this barbarian game or even himself. Since he was learning about combat and weapons literally on the run, hightailing it was a *strategy*, not an act of cowardice.

He pulled up to catch his breath. Before he could turn, he heard the gladiator's footsteps, like the crunching of cereal between molars. He spun, swinging his sword in time to deflect his opponent's blade. Sparks snapped between them. The man leaned in, howling in rage. Rancid breath filled Xander's nostrils. The man's eyes were black, hateful.

Xander caught movement beneath him. The gladiator was reaching beneath their sword arms. His hand grabbed at Xander's torso, much the way David's had done not so long ago, but so very far away. This time, however, Xander's skin was slick with sweat. The man's fingers could not get a grip. Xander pulled his sword back. It came off the gladiator's weapon and dropped onto the top of his forearm. It sliced a deep groove into the man's flesh. Xander continued the movement of his hand until his sword was positioned over his head, ready to bring it down.

Xander knew the gladiator's entire life had been about surviving in battle. He would not be defeated so easily. Xander caught a flash of the man's sword as it swung up. If nothing changed, it would catch Xander below the ribcage and angle diagonally through his chest to his heart. Abandoning the possibility of victory, as close as the lashing down of his hand, Xander pitched himself sideways. He somersaulted, was up, scurrying away again.

That image of his heart impaled on the gladiator's blade made him sick and dizzy. It did not stoke the fire of determination. Rather, an overwhelming sense of defeat washed over him. It occurred to him this was how battles were won and lost. They were not always the result of superior skill and stamina. Close calls, images of impending death, and the lack of opportunities were just as instrumental in putting combatants in the ground. Xander suspected that with experience, a fighter became accustomed to these little defeats; so he would reach the point of giving up much later than Xander would.

Giving up? No, he was not there yet. He did, however, doubt his chances of getting out of this alive. After all, he was a fifteen-year-old boy, living a relatively cushy life by most standards. His opponent had lived a brutal life in a brutal world—he was a shark: Xander nothing but a minnow.

But even minnows wanted to live.

The gladiator huffed toward him. If the nicks Xander had inflicted to the man's shins had enraged him, the slice to his arm and perhaps Xander's escape had sent him into a stratosphere of maniacal hatred. Despite his wounds, the man moved faster. His sword sliced the air before him, this way and that.

In seventh grade, Xander had fought a kid who was smaller than he was. Xander hadn't wanted a showdown, couldn't even remember what had ticked the kid off. He'd easily parried some blows. Finally, to end it, he gave the boy a hard knock on the side of his head. Instead of admitting defeat, the kid had come at him with wild disregard for anything except pummeling Xander. Xander had discovered that pinwheeling arms were nearly impossible to stop. They just kept coming like a lumber mill's saw, and you were the tree.

The gladiator was coming at him like that. With swords, though, instead of scrawny seventh-grader fists.

The blades moved so fast they left gleaming arcs in the

air that appeared solid to Xander. He could hear them now, hissing through the air like the mace never had. Rage may have pushed the gladiator into this mulcher mentality, but he had not lost any dexterity in reaching it. The blades whirled in perfect opposition to each other. One coming up as the other came down. They crossed in front of the man and never so much as grazed each other.

Xander backed away. He made feeble slashes at the approaching *Pinwheel of Death*. Xander wondered how, at a time like this, he could name the instrument of his own demise like that. Definitely too many movies. Too many movie posters and trailers, with their catchphrases and taglines.

"Stop!" he yelled. "This isn't fair." He continued moving backward, keeping ten feet between him and the whirling blades. He stepped on something, twisted his ankle, almost fell. He steadied himself, lifted his leg higher, and stepped back. He had almost tripped over another body. He didn't want to see it; he'd join its former owner soon enough.

The gladiator continued after him. That nasty sneer never left his face. He could have moved in for the kill at any time. Xander thought this drawn-out prelude to his dissection was orchestrated. The gladiator was as much a performer as warrior. Xander hoped his body parts would not teleport back to the house. It was bad enough to die this way. Torturing his family with evidence of it was cosmically cruel. If his parts did make it home, would it be David who discovered them? Would they splash down at his feet back in the little room? True, it would keep his kid brother from making Xander's mistake, but could you ever recover from seeing something like that?

Xander was backing toward a wall. Soon, the only thing left for the gladiator to do was end this performance. Xander swung his sword again and again. If nothing else, he would go out fighting.

When he could reverse no farther, he screamed, another unintelligible representation of his anguish. Then, the sound formed into words—defiant, angry last words: "Come on, you fat pig! Do it!"

The blades whirled. His own weapon clashed against them. *Chang! Chang!* His wrist snapped one way, then the other as the blades battered his sword. For a moment, he wondered if he should pull his arm in so that the first hot cut would be the last he knew. Otherwise, he would watch his hand go first, then his arm, fed slowly into the ancient Roman version of a blender.

Something rumbled. The sounds of the crowd were returning to him. Their feet stomped in anticipation. As his right hand swung the sword, his left counterbalanced the weight. Held out from his side and back just a little, his fingers pressed the hewn stone of the arena wall.

The spinning blades ripped his sword from his grip. It flipped away. Something clamped around his left wrist. He was yanked into the wall, then through the threshold of one of the big wooden doors. He plunged into shadow, as the door rumbled closed. A latch snapped shut. From the other side, swords *thunked* against the wood.

Hands grabbed his shoulders, breath—not rancid, but smelling of toothpaste—blew over him.

"Are you all right?" someone screamed.

His legs felt weak. Emotion, like adrenaline, hit his heart, rushed into his face. He said, "Dad?"

"It's okay, Son. Hold on."

CHAPTER

twenty-nine

As soon as Xander and his father crossed the threshold, the
door slammed shut. Xander's face was pressed into his father's
chest. Dad's arms around him had never felt so good. Xander
opened one eye. He saw the bench and shelf in the small room.
David stood a few feet away. He was shaking and sniffing. His
eyes were puffy and red, still leaking. He had been crying, hard
and long. Xander tried to smile at him. He squeezed even

closer to his father, trying, for just a moment, to get lost in the man's warmth and smell, his very being. He hitched in a stuttering breath. Then he wept. It started gently, then grew into ragged sobs. Too many emotions to hold in. Relief swirled with the residue of intense fear. His *soul* felt abused and tired.

A month before school had let out, Mitch Dawson had been goofing off in his new ride, a '74 Firebird Formula. He had been ripping donuts in the school parking lot. Mitch had lost control, nailed a car, then a light pole. The Firebird had jumped the curb and rolled down the concrete embankment of a runoff canal. The whole school had run out to see. When Xander got there, Mitch was bawling like a baby. Everyone had assumed he was grieving for his totaled car, but later he had confessed to Xander that as the car was rolling, he had been completely and utterly convinced he was going to die. Through an embarrassed smile, he had said, "I stared death in the face and got another chance." Xander had nodded, but had not truly understood. Now he did.

Dad let him cry it out. He stroked Xander's hair and whispered over and over, "You're here now."

When the worst of it was over, he felt David hug him from behind. The boy slid around to include their father in the embrace. They stayed like that a long while. When Xander raised his head, David released them and Xander took a step back. He wiped at his cheeks and ran the underside of his nose over his forearm. He sniffed back what hadn't already come out. He said, "I'm sorry."

Dad squeezed his shoulder. "I am so glad you're here."

Xander glanced at David, back to Dad. "But how . . ."

"Your brother came and got me." He offered David a tight, I'm-proud-of-you smile.

Xander turned to David. He couldn't help it. He had to hug him.

David returned the squeeze, but said, "Are we a bunch of girls or what?"

"Shut up."

When Xander released him, David didn't let go. "Man, I thought you were gone forever."

"So did I. I couldn't find the . . . Dad, how did you follow me?" Then he noticed the animal pelt tied around his father's waist over his pajama bottoms. The sword Dae had been holding was in the scabbard, slung around Dad's neck, hanging under his arm. Xander had a faint memory of feeling it as he embraced his father, but he had been too lost in his emotions to care what it was.

"I couldn't get the door open," David explained. "It locked me out. Dad put those things on and opened it."

Xander said, "How did you know to do that?"

"David told me how the door opened after you put on the chain mail and helmet." He shrugged. "Not difficult to figure out."

"But why didn't you end up where I did, in the middle of the arena?"

Dad's eyebrows went up. "You can add that to my long list of questions, Xander."

"Where *did* you appear?"

"In the bleachers, on the other side of where I got you. I went through, and suddenly I was standing in the middle of a crowd that was chanting for someone's death. I almost croaked myself when I saw it was you."

Xander squinted at him. "They were chanting *sign*-something. You know it?"

"*Sine missione*. It means 'to the death.' Romans used to say it to encourage the winning gladiators to take down their opponents."

"Dad, we were in the *Colosseum!*"

"I recognized it."

"Like in Rome?" David said, catching the excitement.

"But it was *new*," Xander told his father. "Like it was twenty centuries ago."

"History is my subject, Son. Good thing I studied the Colosseum. I knew there were tunnels under the arena. When I saw where you were heading, I used them to reach the door closest to you."

"Just in time," Xander said and felt his eyes tear up again.

"Just in time?" David said. "What happened?"

Xander opened his mouth to answer but simply couldn't. He didn't know where to start, how much to say . . . "Was that real?" he asked his father.

"Felt real to *me*. And . . ." Dad poked Xander's arm.

Xander flinched away. "Ahhh."

A long swath of skin had been flayed from his bicep. It was glistening red. Blood had trickled down to his elbow.

"Ow!" David said for him.

Dad said, "Talk about a close call. You almost lost your arm."

"Arms," Xander corrected. "And legs and head."

"*What?*" David squealed. "How? What happened?"

"I'll tell you later, okay?"

David had moved beyond the terrible panic he must have felt at Xander's disappearance. Now he was fired up. But out of respect for his brother's condition, he nodded. He could wait . . . barely.

Dad untied the pelt and hung it from a hook. He slipped the sword and scabbard off his shoulder, hung it on the next hook. "These things," he said. "I'm not sure how, but I think they helped us get back." He studied them, hanging on the hooks, swinging gently back and forth. "When I got to your side of the Colosseum, they got . . . I don't know, *heavier.* I realized they hadn't gained pounds, but they were pulling away from me, like they were trying to go somewhere. When I grabbed you, I kind of went with them, let them tug me where they wanted to."

"Tug?" David said. "That pelt and sword were tugging *you?*"

Dad nodded. "That's what it was, a tug. When I gave into it, we fell back and landed here."

"So the items are what get you there and bring you back?" Xander said.

"I don't know if they bring you back or simply show you the way. Maybe we were close to the portal anyway, and they led us to it." He eyed Xander funny. "David said you had chain mail."

"And a helmet," Xander said. "I left them back in the arena. Now that you say it, the chain mail did get heavy; that's why I dropped it. Maybe it was tugging me toward the portal." His face paled. "If I needed them to get back . . . and I lost them . . . I could have been stuck there." His eyes welled with tears again. "If you hadn't come for me . . ."

Dad gripped his shoulder. "It's okay. We're here now, that's all that matters."

"Except for not helping me get back," Xander said, "is it bad I lost them? Nothing bad will happen because I didn't bring them back, will it?"

Dad shook his head. "No more questions, Xander." He lifted his foot onto the bench, leaned an arm over his knee. "I have a question for the two of you, though."

Here it comes, Xander thought. *The lecture, the scolding.* He and David exchanged a look.

Their dad said, "Chocolate or vanilla?"

If he had suddenly slapped David, he could not have elicited a more stunned expression on the boy's face.

Xander stumbled over his words. "But . . . what . . . uh . . . Don't you want to talk to us about . . . all of *this*?" He swept his hands in a wide arc trying to encompass this room, all the rooms, the hidden stairway and corridor.

Dad scrunched his brow. "We'll get to that. But let's get some sleep first. And, of course, ice cream."

"Since you put it that way," Xander said, "chocolate."

CHAPTER

thirty

It was only a dream, Xander thought. He blinked against the sun coming through the bedroom windows.

Then he rolled over, and the wound on his arm flared with white-hot pain.

"Aaahhh!"

David stirred under his covers. He turned to face Xander. "Hurt?"

"No, I always wake up screaming." He turned the clock radio toward him. 10:13. Yow. Dad must have asked Mom to let them sleep in. She was usually all over them if they weren't up "before the sun got hot." He said, "I thought I'd dreamed the whole thing, fighting a gladiator in the Roman Colosseum."

David shook his head. "It wasn't a dream. I was there when you went . . . and when Dad brought you back."

Xander closed his eyes. Thinking about it made his stomach sour. All those bodies. His own close shave with death. Even the simple fact that life's rules—especially the ones dealing with time and space, little things like these—were not carved in stone, as he had been taught. All of it made him feel disoriented, like a kite broken from its string, whipping around in the wind. He'd just woken up, and already he was getting a headache.

"Xander, what happened over there? You said Dad got there just in time."

He didn't open his eyes.

"Are you going to tell me?"

"David, it wasn't good. Trust me, you don't want to know."

"I want to try it."

Xander's lids flipped open. "It?"

"Going someplace. Through the door."

"No, you don't want to try it. Don't say that."

"Dad did it and came right back. He wasn't in any danger."

"David, I almost died."

"But you *didn't.*" His eyes sparkled with excitement.

"I didn't know you were so stupid."

David's smile faltered. Xander reminded himself that Dae had saved his life last night. If he hadn't fetched their father, Xander would have been slaughtered by that barbarian. In fact, he would have been in his grave for about two thousand years by now. That was something to think about.

Xander blinked slowly. "Sorry. I'm just saying I don't know why you would even be thinking this way, when you saw what happened to me."

"I didn't *see.* That's just it."

"Well, I'm telling you, okay? I almost died, and it was the most horrible experience of my life."

David considered this. After a time, he said, "I'm not talking about going where you went. Just *somewhere.*"

Xander threw his legs out from under the covers and sat up. He thought of David and the situation he had been in, under the shield as the sword came down on it. He wouldn't have had the physical strength to survive. Nothing against him, just his age. And all those bodies . . . Xander wasn't sure how well *he* was going to handle it over time. He got up and sat on David's bed. "I know it sounds exciting; I would think that too. But it's not worth it."

David looked like he had been told Christmas had been called off. He said, "You and Dad got to do it."

"If we'd been in a car accident, would you want to do that too?"

"That's different."

"It's *not* different, David. That's what I'm trying to tell you. It's just as scary and potentially deadly. When Dad brought me back, the first thing I thought of was a friend who'd been in a car accident. I'm telling you, that's what it was like."

David's face reflected his disappointment. Xander could tell he wasn't totally convinced.

Xander said, "Promise me you won't sneak off and do it."

David said nothing.

"*Promise* me."

David's lips grew tight. The bottom one rolled out a little. His stubborn face.

"If you don't promise, I'm gonna follow you every second of every day. Even to the bathroom. I'll be like a bad smell you can't wash away."

Slowly, a smile found David's face. He said, "I promise."

"Okay." Xander pushed him playfully on the chest. He stood. He snatched his jeans off a post at the foot of the bed and pulled them on. He had showered the night before, which was really earlier that morning. He could not believe how much grime and dirt and blood the water had sluiced off him to swirl down the drain. His father had stayed with him, leaning against the sink, talking quietly. Xander knew Dad was worried about him. He had seen some of what Xander had gone through. He had also commented that he hoped the jaunt itself, to another time and place, did not have lasting consequences on their physical bodies or mental state. Xander should have reminded David of that, but he had gotten him to promise and that was all that mattered right then. Dad had said they would decide what to do about the rooms upstairs another time. For now, they were off-limits. He had also asked the boys to not tell Mom or Toria. He was afraid they would panic and want to leave without carefully considering the situation, and since the corridor was behind a secret wall, there was no need to stir up trouble.

"Let sleeping dogs lie," Dad had said.

It bothered Xander that in the short time since their move, the number of secrets in their family had skyrocketed.

"What are you going to tell Mom?" David asked, seeming to know Xander's thoughts. This was one of the topics he and Dad had discussed while he let the hot shower strip centuries-old dirt off his body. When he'd come to bed after that, David had already been asleep.

He looked at the gauze and tape Dad had applied. "Just an accident while investigating the house."

David sat up in bed. "You're going to flat-out *lie*?"

Xander pulled on a T-shirt. His movements made his arm throb. "It's not really lying. We *were* investigating the house, and it *was* an accident." He registered David's expression and sighed. "I know, I know. If it's not a lie, it's darn close. Dad said sometimes lies told to keep people safe are okay."

"Hmm. Do you think Dad has lied to us?"

Xander pulled a pair of socks from his drawer and picked up his sneakers. He'd put them on outside, on the front porch steps. He wanted to spend more time outside today. He shook his head. "I think Dad's as straight as they come."

David smiled.

As he left the room, Xander thought, *What's one more lie?*

CHAPTER

thirty-one

After breakfast, Xander decided he needed fresh air and sunshine. He and David set off to explore their property.

Every few minutes Xander found himself looking back through the trees at the house. He kept expecting to see something not right: an angle or addition that wasn't true; or, as before, a whole chunk of house just up and gone. If the house played tricks, it wasn't doing it today. The irregular

squeak-squeak of the weathervane on top of the tower continually reminded him of its looming presence.

They'd been out awhile, and his hunger told him it was close
to lunchtime. Some time ago David had wandered off toward
the back while Xander explored the dense forest on one side
of the house. Bushes and trees had gone unpruned for decades.
Even at midday the area was cloaked in shadow. Enough sunlight seeped through to render flashlights unnecessary, but no
one would mistake Xander's trek through the bush for a cheery
walk in the park. Most interesting to him were the fallen trees.
They lay here and there in various stages of decomposition.
Rolling them over, when they were small enough or decayed
enough, revealed swarming worlds of beetles and centipedes,
spiders and worms. He always tried to find the stump of a
fallen tree. Sometimes it was nearby. Other times he'd have to
walk around to find it, usually up an embankment. He'd make
up stories about how the trees fell: lightning, beavers, some
dudes fooling around with an ax. Probably most had simply
died and fallen over. But that was boring.

He had his camera out now and was filming a black beetle
crawl over one of Toria's dolls in macro-lens mode when he heard
David calling him. He kept the camera rolling and brought the
camera up to capture his brother's progress through the woods.
David moved toward him, stepping into and out of shafts of
light, into and out of view. Then he veered away, still calling.

Xander considered letting him wander completely out of

sight and out of earshot. That would make a funny short film, if a bit abstract. Deciding against being mean today, he yelled, "Over here!"

"Come see something," David said, leaping over bushes and deadfalls to reach him.

"What is it?" Xander asked.

David puzzled at the overturned log and Toria's Barbie. Ants were swarming over her face, through her hair. "What are you doing?" he asked.

Xander smiled. "The doll represents Average Man—or Woman. The bugs are all the little problems that plague him. See?"

"I think I liked it better when you were making movies about skateboarders wiping out."

"I am now *le artiste*," Xander said, trying to sound as French as François Truffaut. He raised his fingers to the sky, in a flourish, thinking he looked flamboyant and artsy. He was enjoying the dual distractions of the outdoors and his cinematic aspirations.

His brother thought about that. He said, "Whatever. Come see what I found."

"Is it cool?"

"It's weird."

Xander paused. He wasn't so sure he could take any more weirdness.

"Not like last night," David assured him. "Kind of . . . just *weird*. It won't make you think you're crazy or anything." Then: "I don't think it will."

"Lead the way," Xander said.

They pushed deeper into the woods, behind the house. At times, the bushes and brambles, trees and branches were so thick they had to walk around as surely as they would a mountain. Xander watched the house recede, becoming less distinct through all the foliage. After a time, he could see it no more. The shadows were even darker here. It made Xander think of the Hansel and Gretel woods, how they got lost in them. More accurately, it resembled the woods in every werewolf movie he'd ever seen.

"How much farther?" he asked.

"Just up here."

"How'd you get this far away from the house?" David had ventured at least three times the distance Xander had.

"I thought I heard something."

"Like what?"

"Footsteps. You know, breaking branches and crunching."

"Footsteps? Out here?"

"And then laughing."

Xander stopped. "David, with everything we've gone through, you followed footsteps and laughter into the creepiest woods we've ever seen?"

David shrugged. "I didn't think anything would happen outside the house. It wasn't spooky laughter. More like . . ." He thought about it. "A kid on a playground."

"You haven't seen enough movies. Children are a vital part

of ghost stories. They lure you in, then *wham!*" He punched his fist into his palm.

David shook his head. He turned and kept going. Xander hesitated, then followed.

"See there?" David said.

Through the trees ahead, sunlight broke through. It wasn't a mere shaft but a radiant glow covering a wide area. A clearing.

Xander thought if David had found a stone altar, he was going back to the motel, with or without everybody else.

But when he stepped out of what had become an impossibly dense forest, he was both fascinated and puzzled. Fascinated because out of untamed wilderness was a meadow half the size of a football field. The ground was mostly flat and covered in a thick, green grass. No rocks, bushes, or trees marred its parklike perfection. It was shaped like an egg, its boundaries well-defined by the dark, imposing forest that completely surrounded it. Overhead, the canopy of the treetops leaned way in, forming a natural dome. At the center, an opening revealed blue sky, white clouds.

The strangest aspect of this area could not be seen, only felt. It was as though Xander had instantly ascended to the top of a high mountain. The air was cooler and felt thinner. It rushed into his lungs with ease, giving him a mild jolt of energy. When Xander was David's age, oxygen bars were all the rage. Dad was curious and took him to one. They held masks over their mouths and noses and breathed from a canister of oxygen, like you see in hospitals. Both of them had decided the gimmick was a rip-off. However, the purchased air did somehow *taste* better than regular air and had made them morning-perky. The air in the meadow felt— *tasted*—like that.

"What is this?" Xander asked.

David shook his head. "Can't be natural, can it?"

At first, Xander had thought the same thing. Now he saw imperfections humans wouldn't leave—the ground under the grass was bumpy, wavy; the trees encroached into the area just enough to give the perimeter a slightly shabby appearance. Despite the unmistakable dome of the leafy canopy, there was no evidence any pruning had occurred. If someone had carved the clearing from the forest, it had not been tended to in a long time.

As Xander's eyes scanned upward, David said, "But that's not all."

Xander laughed. His brother had stepped out twenty feet into the meadow. "Say that again," he said.

"I said, that's not all."

"Why are you talking like that?"

"Like what?"

"Your voice. It's higher pitched." David's voice had not yet started changing. When he answered the phone, people still mistook him for their mother and sometimes even Toria. While not dramatic, his voice was even higher now.

Xander walked toward him. "I've listened to you enough to know what you sound—" As he spoke, the pitch of his own voice rose. Not to an unnatural level, but the way it did when he got excited or whiny about something. "Hello? Hello? Hear that?"

"I'm talking right now," David said. He was listening to his own voice, nodding, an open-mouthed grin widening with each word.

Xander said, "Can you hear it in me?"

"Yeah!" David started howling like a wolf. His pitch rose to ear-splitting, glass-breaking levels.

"All right, all right," Xander said, covering his ears. "Stop it."

"Now look," David said, He ran out into the meadow, then back.

"Okay?" Xander said.

"What'd I do?"

Xander looked at him from the corner of his eye. "You . . . ran."

"How fast?"

"All-out sprint, dude." And then he noticed David was not out of breath. He said, "Wasn't it?"

David shook his head. "I was jogging. Now watch this." He walked away. He ran past Xander at a pretty good clip, but nothing stunning. Then he jumped. A little too high, a little too far. It was nothing most people would probably notice. But this close, and knowing him so well, Xander knew it wasn't normal. Xander took off across the field. He didn't feel like Dash, the fast kid in *The Incredibles*. It simply felt like a good run on a good day. He leaped into the air. From his own perspective, he realized it was the best jump of his life.

Directly in front of him, a man climbed through the brambles and stepped into the clearing. Xander braked and fell back onto his butt.

It was Dad. He had leaves in his hair. One sleeve of his sweatshirt was pushed up over his elbow, the other down around his wrist. Sweat had soaked through in the shape of his sternum.

"Xander," Dad said. He sounded excited. Then Xander realized it was a casual greeting, and the excited part was the tricky air making his voice higher than normal.

His father reached him and held out a hand to help him up.

As Xander rose, he said, "What are you doin' here?"

David ran up and stood by his brother's side.

"Out looking for you," Dad said. "I've got to run some errands, and I'd like you boys to stay in the house."

Xander realized Dad had not commented on the clearing at all, let alone the strangeness of the air and the way it affected their voices. "How did you come from over there?" he asked his father, pointing. It was the opposite direction from the house.

Dad looked over his shoulder as if just catching that. He said, "I heard you guys, but you know how sounds are around here. Must have gotten lost."

"Must have gotten *really* lost," David said. He reached up and pulled a leafy twig out of Dad's hair.

Dad smiled. "Are these crazy woods, or what?"

Xander said, "Were you out this way earlier today?"

"The other day I was. Found this clearing." He looked around in wonder, shook his head.

"What do you think this place is?" David said.

"More weirdness, Dae. But pretty lightweight stuff, compared. You know?" He winked.

Xander knew what he meant. Still, it bothered him to find yet another oddity on their property. It was like all the anomalies of the world had congregated on this one spot. Or—more likely—one truly weird abnormality happened here and smaller drops of strangeness splattered out from it. He pictured a dollop of paint falling from God's palette, striking the earth where the house now stood. Its splatter made things like this clearing and who knew what else?

As Dad passed them, he gave David a healthy shove. The kid fell and tumbled—farther than he should have, laughing all the way.

CHAPTER

thirty-two

When Xander returned from a late-night bathroom run,
David was not in his bed. The covers were folded back, exposing only sheets and a pillow. Had he been there when Xander
got up? *Yeah*, he thought. He remembered hearing David's
rhythmic breathing. It was only a little after eleven, but the
day spent outside had worn them out. The boys had crashed
around ten. Xander had watched the shadows on the ceiling,

falling in and out of light sleep until he realized he had to visit the bathroom. Maybe David had felt the same need, and finding the bathroom occupied, went to one of the others.

"David," he whispered, in case the boy was hiding. No answer. Xander crawled in bed, pulled the cover over his shoulder, closed his eyes. They snapped open again. He threw back his blankets and jumped up.

"David?" he said, louder. "*Oh no!*"

He ran from the room and down the hall. Past the foyer. Past their parents' bedroom to where the hallway bent and went toward the back of the house. By the illumination of the night-light, he saw the false wall was angled into the hallway, leaving a gap of several feet.

"David!"

He ran through, scraping his injured arm on the edge. He felt the pain, but did not allow it to distract him. The second door, the one with the metal skin, was also open. He slammed into the doorjamb, rolled off and through, and started up the stairs. A flashlight clicked on, blinding him.

"David?"

"What took you so long?" He was sitting on the landing.

"What are you *doing?*" Xander's concern had instantly turned to anger.

"I promised I wouldn't go into the rooms without you."

"Then what are you doing?" Xander repeated.

"Waiting for you. I can come here any time I want. See?"

"What are you saying?"

"I want to know what it's like. Just once."

"David, there is no way—"

"Just once, Xander. You can help me, or not."

"You promised."

"I'm not breaking it, but I'll take it back if you don't help."

Xander's heart felt squeezed to the size of a raisin. David was honest, but that did not always translate into being *good*.

"Scoot over," Xander said. He sat beside his brother. While David played the light over the stairs, the open door below and, occasionally, down the hotel-like corridor, Xander told him about fighting the gladiator. He did not spare any detail. The bodies. The sword crashing down on the shield. The soldiers who attacked when he had begged them for help. The close calls, when he'd thought he was dead. David listened without making a sound. When Xander finished, they sat quietly. David had stilled his hand; the light shined on his sneakers.

After a few minutes, Xander felt his brother's hand on his shoulder. David said, "I'm sorry that happened to you."

"You see why I don't want you to do it?"

At first, David didn't reply. Then he whispered, "I have to. If I don't, I'll always wonder. My whole life."

"If you do, your whole life may not be very long." Xander had to admit this was consistent with David's personality. He had dirt biked and scuba dived, hit a black diamond slope on only their fourth trip to Mammoth Mountain, and had even flown in an ultralight with a friend's father. Xander was into adventure as well, but never with David's degree of enthusiasm—Dad called it "reckless abandon." David could ramble on for hours about the things he wanted to do when he became old enough: pilot a jet; bungee from some bridge on the Zimbabwe-Zambia border; and streetluge, which was like putting wheels on your back and flying down the longest, scariest road you could find. Once, when the dinnertime conversation turned to how each of them wanted to die, Xander had said "In my sleep." *Yeah, that sounded like a decent way to go.*

David had said, "I want to hang glide into a cliff when I'm ninety." *OK, that was cool,* Xander had admitted to himself. Then David had added, in all seriousness, "Or get eaten by a shark." He did not have a death wish. He would be the first to say he wanted to live a long, long time, so he could do all the things he dreamed about doing. It was more like, for David, life was most exciting when you could lose it. Xander didn't think David had actually figured that out yet. But it was true.

Now that Xander thought about it, he had been an idiot to think he could keep David out of those rooms. His little brother got scared like everyone did. He was just very adept at pushing his fear aside when doing so led to some grand new adventure.

"Look," Xander said, "if I go along with it, I pick which room."

"Not something stupid, like the one with the beach towel."

"That one sounds like a lot of fun to me."

David just looked at him.

Xander said, "Okay, but nothing with a weapon. Okay? A weapon seems like a bad sign."

"Well, if the only rooms that look cool are the ones with weapons . . ."

"No," Xander said. "No weapons, no matter what." When David didn't respond, he added, "Otherwise, I'll drag your butt to Dad right now. He'll brick up that wall down there, and if that doesn't work, I'll kick and scream till we move."

"All right, already. No weapons."

Before his brother's agreement had registered in Xander's mind, David was standing, stepping toward the corridor. He flipped the switch, turning on the lights.

Xander stepped up behind him. "Do you know which room?"

"Antechamber."

"What?"

"That's what Dad called these rooms: *antechambers*."

"Whatever. Do you know which one?"

David shook his head. Xander stepped past David and opened the first door.

"That's the beach towel room," David complained.

"Uh . . . no it's not." Hanging from the hooks were an astronaut's helmet, a metallic space suit, something that looked like a pistol, but may have been a welding torch. There were a few other items consistent with an outer-space adventure.

"Whoa," David said, looking past Xander.

Xander quickly said, "There's a gun. That's a weapon."

"That's not a weapon!"

"I said, not this one." Xander slammed the door.

He opened it again, peered in. He clicked it shut, once more. He said, "You know, I think you're right. That *was* the beach towel room."

"Duh. Those beach things with the flip-flops were the first things we saw. Remember?"

Xander nodded. "Well . . . it changed."

David scrunched his nose, hitched up his top lip. "Would Dad do that?"

"Why would he? And . . ." Xander thought about it. "It's not like someone just switched the things around, and I don't remember seeing astronaut stuff. I *know* we checked every room."

David nodded in agreement. "Somebody put *brand-new* stuff in there."

Simultaneously, they gazed up the corridor at the other doors. About ten minutes later, they had rechecked every room. About half of the themes were ones they had seen the previous night, though both brothers thought they were in different rooms. The other themes were altogether new.

"Who's doing it, you think?" David asked.

Xander was squinting at the doors. "I don't know, but . . ." They went to every room again, verifying that none of the themes had changed since their last inspection. None had.

"Maybe they all change at a specific time," Xander suggested. "Or when no one's around."

They were silent for a while. At last, David clapped his hands together. He strolled up the center of the carpeted runner. "Let's see. Which one . . . had . . ." Thinking, thinking. "The police badge and uniform?"

"No weapons," Xander reminded him.

"That one didn't have . . . oh, the pistol."

"You'd probably wind up smack in the middle of a bank robbery."

Xander caught the spark in David's eye before he turned away.

"David . . ."

"I know. How about that one with the rope and carabiners?"

Xander tossed his hands up. "You don't know how to mountain climb! These places don't suddenly give you new skills. They just drop you in."

David opened a door. He turned a smile on Xander, then stepped through.

"What?" Xander said, rushing to catch the door before it shut.

Khaki-colored safari hat. Compass. A vest with many pockets and loops and straps. A canteen on a utility belt. A machete. On the bench were knee-high leather boots.

"A jungle?" Xander said.

David grinned and nodded.

Xander said, "A *machete*. That's a weapon."

"It's a tool. I'll probably have to cut my way out of some bushes, that's all."

Xander didn't like it, but a deal was a deal. He pulled the utility belt off its hook and held it out to David.

The boy hesitated. When he reached for it, his hand trembled.

Xander's eyebrows went up. "You okay?"

"Yeah." His voice was high, like it had been in the clearing. His tongue clicked dryly in his mouth.

Xander thought of Richard Dreyfuss in *Jaws*, when he was preparing to go in the shark cage. He was so afraid he couldn't spit into his diving mask to keep it from fogging up. Now there was a David personality for you: scared, but willing to do it anyway.

David cinched the belt around his waist. Xander handed him the machete. He unsheathed it and gave it the once-over. He clipped it to the belt. Xander set the helmet on his brother's head. It was too big and made him look five years old.

"Dad's gonna kill me," Xander said.

David reached for the second door's handle.

"Wait!" Xander said. "Don't open that door. I'll be right back."

"What?" David said.

"Just wait, don't move." Xander hurried out of the room. Even with reining in his speed on the stairs and tiptoeing past the master bedroom, he reached his and Dae's room and was back in the antechamber upstairs in no more than a minute. He held his camcorder up to David. "Here, take this."

"I don't want that!" David protested. "What if I need my hands? What if I lose it?"

Xander let the camera drop to the end of its long leather strap. He slipped it over David's head so it hung around his neck.

"I'll turn it on now," he said, flipping the power switch and pushing the record button. "If you think about it, point it at something. If you don't, we'll still have proof you went somewhere. You might not want to burp or do anything too embarrassing, though."

"Like scream?" David asked. He opened the inner door.

The antechamber instantly became more humid. A botanical fragrance wafted in. Beyond the threshold, fat, green leaves swayed in a breeze. Trees rose out of sight, hairy-looking vines looped down, almost touching the moss-covered earth.

"You sure about this?" Xander asked.

David nodded. He tightened the helmet strap under his chin.

Xander said, "How long was I gone last night?"

David shrugged. "Twenty minutes?"

"So, it's probably all in real time. A minute over there is a minute here. If you're not back in fifteen minutes, I'm gonna get Dad and come after you."

David nodded. He stepped through.

The door pulled out of Xander's grip and slammed shut.

CHAPTER

thirty-three

David watched the door waver and fade away. The moist heat drew sweat from his face and neck. The plants seemed to quiver, but whether from wind or some kind of ground tremor, David didn't know. The cushy grasses and moss prevented him from feeling much else under his feet. A bird cawed in the distance. It was a sound like an alarm that set David's nerves on edge. He was already thinking about how he would get back. If the door had vanished, where would he find the portal to home? He did want to experience this world, but he would have felt a lot better knowing where the exit was. He trusted that *somehow*—either with Xander's help or as Dad had said, through some signal from the items he held—the portal would reveal itself.

He stepped to the fern where the door had shimmered and ceased to be. He was moving the leaves around when a centipede—as long as his arm and as thick as a hotdog—scuttled up the frond toward his hand. Its front half rose up, as if to look David in the eyes. Its many legs wiggled and waved. Huge pincers, coming off its head, clamped and opened, clamped and opened. Unsure if the thing could leap or how fast it could move if it decided David looked like a tasty treat, he reversed another few steps. His heel crunched on something. A brown and yellow beetle, as big as an egg, oozed yellow guts from its shattered shell. Three others, bigger, moved quickly toward David, perhaps intent on avenging their friend. He gingerly danced away on tiptoes.

Should have put on the boots, he thought. He backed into something that moved easily under David's touch: a long, fat snake, hanging from a branch. David yelled, then laughed at himself: it was only a vine. He sighed, then spotted a real snake, slithering down the vine in his direction. Having already yelled, he bit his tongue and backed away.

His heart was a ferret, caged within his chest, panicky to get out. It seemed to jump and twirl and bang against his breastbone and his ribs. Its frantic beats made little room for the expansion of his lungs, and he found breathing to be difficult.

Well away from the snake and centipede and beetles, he stopped. He scanned the area, saw no immediate threats. He closed his eyes and forced himself to take a long, deep breath. He lifted Xander's camera off his stomach, where it had been bouncing at the end of its strap. He made sure the Record light was on, then held it to his face. He zoomed in on the vine and snake, panned to the plant where the centipede had been. He didn't see it now, in the camera's little LCD screen.

Nearby, something roared. It was a big animal, a wild cat. David lowered the camera. It roared again, and he wondered if it had caught his scent and was crooning its excitement about finding an exotic meal.

As if in answer, a second animal roared, in the opposite direction, but seeming just as near. The next roar came from a third beast—between the first two, but farther off. That ferret in his chest had found his throat and was pushing up into it.

David shook his head. Considering Xander's experience, it was just like that house to drop him into big-cat territory. From the roars, he figured he was in their favorite feeding zone and it was dinnertime. For all he knew, the portal issued a frequency only tigers could hear—the big-cat equivalent of a dinner bell. He had thought *tiger*, but he didn't know their roars from any of the other big cats. At one time or another, he had heard them all at the San Diego Zoo, but he wasn't nerd enough about animals to distinguish the difference. He thought he had read somewhere—or maybe it was from the singing animals in *The Jungle Book*—that the only big cats in jungle settings were leopards, panthers, and tigers. The roars were throaty and loud. Had to be tigers.

Whatever they were, he didn't want to hang around to find out. He unsheathed the machete. Its weight felt good in his hand. He admired its gleaming edge.

One of the beasts roared again. Almost immediately, it received an answering call. Both seemed closer, and David realized how awfully true his statement to Xander had been: the machete was a tool, not a weapon.

He held still, willing it or the hat or the utility belt to show him the way to the portal. He felt nothing, no tug, no weightiness in one direction or another. Maybe he had to move, get closer to the portal before the items started drawing him toward it.

He swung the machete down into a leaf the size and thickness of a bath towel. It fell away before him and he smiled. He sliced again and again, stepping forward each time.

Blazing a path, he thought. *Isn't that what they say?* So he blazed. He had no clue where he would end up, but he believed he was putting ground between him and the tigers. He swung the machete diagonally, lopping away a leaf and a branch. They fell to the ground, revealing the snarling face of a tiger. Its head was huge, twice the size of David's. The cat was pulled back onto its haunches. One paw up, ready to strike.

Its claws were curved blades: a single one could cause butcher-knife damage; five would take off his face and open him up.

He jumped back, but amazingly did not scream. He could not even breathe. He raised the machete over his head and turned it so the big cat could see it. It hissed, baring teeth the size of railroad spikes. Its eyes watched David intently.

He had heard something about what *not* to do with great predators. If he remembered right, turning and running would be the end of him. Rather, he backed slowly away. The animal did not move. Reversing along the path he had blazed, he moved around a bend and lost sight of the beast. Almost directly behind him, lost among the heavy leaves, another tiger roared.

Certainly not the same one. It could not have—

Finishing his thought for him, the tiger in front roared.

The third tiger joined in, off to his left. David's entire body shook in fear.

Dang it, Xander, he thought, *you could be wrong sometimes, you know.*

With no other place to go, he turned right and pushed through the tangle of vines and branches and plants with their stupid bath-towel leaves. He avoided using the machete, thinking its rhythmic chopping would bring the tigers more quickly, the way a thrashing fish drew sharks. For just a moment, he thought of the centipede and snake and wondered if he'd run into more of *them.* Just as quickly, he dismissed the thought. Those things were just pests in a world of true killers. He *wished* the creepy-crawlers were all he had to worry about.

Unable to cross a particularly dense spot, he chopped at it with the machete. A tiger roared. It sounded close. Leaves rustled nearby. Something was moving alongside him, twenty feet away. He pushed forward and it moved again, pacing him.

He realized he had been hearing the thunderous sound of a waterfall. For a time, he had mistaken it for his own blood rushing past his ears. Hope welled in him. A waterfall meant water, and cats didn't like water. He pushed toward it, chopping and cutting when he had to. He hoped none of the cats realized what he was doing and cut him off.

Something moved, heavy and fast, behind him. He spun, machete raised, expecting to see only the gaping maw of a tiger as it leaped at him. Instead, furry striped hindquarters and a tail flashed past. The thing had run right past him. He didn't know if tigers tormented their prey or if they were simply cautious hunters.

He *felt* tormented and he *felt* hunted.

Then the jungle stopped—just like that. It gave way to the granite edge of a cliff. Way down below, a river sparkled. The waterfall he'd heard was a half-mile away. The other side of the chasm was a long way off.

And the tigers were very close.

Like a gift from heaven, only a stone's throw away, was a bridge spanning the chasm. It was made of rope and wooden planks. If he beat the tigers across it, he could cut the ropes on the other side, separating them from their meal.

A tiger roared . . . David thought it sounded like a laugh. He hurried along the rock ledge to the bridge.

Movement behind him. A snapped twig, leaves flung aside with the sound of a wind-rippled sail, the pounding of heavy paws. He stepped onto the first planks, testing them. The wood felt solid, but the bridge was wobbly. He took another tentative step, ready to run if the tigers appeared, but they were nowhere in sight.

What did appear were men on the other side of the bridge. They were dark skinned and scantily dressed. Some kind of aboriginal tribe, David guessed. He did not know where in the world he was or what these people might be called. The three he had first noticed became triple that as they poured from the dense brush. Certainly they were hunters and would want the tigers. In fact, they carried spears and bows and arrows. He hurried toward them. Two of the archers took aim.

David looked back. No animals. Perhaps these hunters had spooked them. One archer released his arrow. David had to duck to avoid being skewered through the head.

"Hey!" he yelled. The camera swung against his chest.

The other archer fired. The arrow sailed a few inches from David's right arm. A spear came next, in a shallow arc designed to impale him. He dropped straight down onto the planks. The camcorder—he'd forgotten all about it—struck him hard in the chin. The machete flipped out of his hand and pinwheeled into the abyss. The spear clattered on the wood behind him. The bridge began to shake. David closed his eyes and gripped the edges. More shaking. The hunters had mounted the bridge and were running toward him in single file.

He lifted a shaking hand to one of the ropes that acted as a handrail for crossers. He pulled himself up and tore quickly away from the approaching hunters.

Ahead, a section of tall fronds whipped back and forth violently, then stopped. A tiger roared.

An arrow whizzed across his shoulder, slicing his T-shirt. It continued on to *thunk* into a tree, where it quivered as though furious about missing its mark.

David stepped off the bridge. He darted left along the rock ledge. A spear struck the ground three feet ahead of him and snapped in two. Each piece spun off in a different direction. Abruptly, he turned and plunged into the jungle. One of the big cats snarled nearby. It thrashed through the underbrush as big and heavy as a car. David veered away from it. Ahead of him a tiger roared.

He stopped. The thrashing continued for another few seconds, then stilled.

Breathing. Panting. Under it was a rolling *rrrrrr*, almost a purr. Not friendly or loving. This was more of a satisfied sound. The creature knew it was going to get what it wanted.

More rustling in front of David. The inhalation and exhalation of a second beast reached his ears. Farther off, the pattering of bare feet on the wood-planked bridge, growing louder. A fat raindrop struck David's head.

Rain, he thought. *Just what I need right now.*

Another drop splattered on his shoulder. He felt it: sticky. He looked up. The third tiger was crouched on a branch high above him. At least for now, it seemed content to watch. He thought that was a particularly feline trait: to watch or play with its food until it grew bored and then the banquet started. He believed his only choice was to break through the jungle and leap off the cliff. He really didn't think he would survive the fall, even if he hit the water far below. But he would rather have that one chance in a million than no chance at all with these tigers and hunters.

But it was too late.

He could barely see over the top of the greenery in front of him. A dark gap, like a thick crack in the surface of a frozen lake, was moving directly for him—a beast was approaching fast, flattening the grass and plants as it came. Behind him, a branch cracked loudly. The breathing became a growl. It grew louder with each pounding step of the beast. From *two* sides, he thought. Three, if the one above gets involved.

I'm going to be torn apart.

He screamed.

Eyes wide, jaw set, Xander pushed out of the bushes in front of David. He grabbed David by the head and yanked him back. The bushes engulfed them.

"Xander! What are you—"

"Shut up and come on." Xander began crawling on his hands and knees. Every few feet he'd stop to pull David closer. The camcorder dragged on the ground, snagging on things, making David yank it with his neck.

Behind them, the tigers were going crazy, growling, roaring, and by the sounds of it, swiping at the jungle with their claws.

"What are we doing?" David whispered, his voice harsh, almost guttural. "Where are we going? There are three tigers—"

"I know," Xander said. He pulled David alongside him, threw his arm over his back, and gave him a squeeze. "Do you feel it? That tug Dad talked about?"

"No, I—" Then he did: a gentle tug on the utility belt as though Xander had his finger looped into it, but he didn't. The helmet too seemed a bit heavier on the upper right side, the same direction the belt was yearning to go. "That way!" he said.

"Right. It has to be close. I *just* stepped out of the antechamber."

They crawled through the underbrush. The tigers roared and hissed and pawed. They knew where their meal was. They were taking their time, enjoying the hunt.

David's helmet grew heavier, pulling his head suddenly to the side. The belt almost yanked his hips past his body.

Xander said, "Here! Hold on!"

The brothers rolled as one and fell into a hole.

thirty-four

SUNDAY, 12:50 A.M.

They crashed onto the wooden floor of the antechamber. The door slammed against David's legs. He shifted them out of the way, and it banged shut. Xander was suddenly on top of him. He had fistfuls of David's T-shirt, and he was shaking him.

"See?" Xander said. He was so close, David felt spit spray his chin. "See? You didn't listen to me and see what happened!"

Tears ran from the corners of David's eyes into the hair at

his temples. He gritted his teeth. He wasn't gonna cry, he wasn't. He wasn't so sure about Xander, though. His brother stopped yelling, but kept his double-fisted grip on David's collar. They stared into each other's eyes. Xander shook his head.

The ferret in David's chest was settling down. It scampered around and around, more slowly with each revolution. He squeezed his eyes shut, expelling the last of his tears. He could weep, probably should. He had almost died in the most horrific way. From the time he crossed the threshold to when Xander pulled him back, he had been terrified. Stalked by tigers. Hunted by humans. Almost knocked off a bridge. By all rights he should be dead.

But he wasn't. He *wasn't*. That's what he held onto. Air filled his lungs. Blood flowed through his veins. His brother was spitting on him. He was alive.

He smiled, a big toothy grin. Into Xander's gaping-stunned-frightened face, he said, "Can I do it again?"

Xander pulled him up several inches, just so he could toss him down. David's head conked against the floor.

Xander said, "Idiot." He pushed himself off of David. He picked up the camcorder, pulled the strap over his brother's head, and dropped onto the bench.

David lay on the floor, breathing hard. He said, "I'm kidding."

"You're still an idiot."

David said, "Thanks for saving me. How much did you see?"

Xander closed his eyes. "I put on the boots and the compass to open the door. At first, it was just colors, greens and browns. I leaned through the door a little more, just until I felt something trying to pull me in, and I could make out trees and leaves and stuff. It was like the portal was stuttering through the jungle, moving in little jerky motions. All of a sudden, I was right next to a *tiger!* I could smell it!"

"There were three of them," David said.

Xander nodded, his eyes still closed. "I could tell there was more than one. I saw a flash of your shirt, but I wasn't sure it was you. I waited to see if it would come around again. But then I was afraid I'd lose you completely, so I stepped through. Not far from you, as it turned out." He examined the camera. It was dirty and scratched. He picked a leaf off it and tossed it to the floor. Immediately the leaf flipped in the air, as though caught in a draft, and fluttered away through the gap at the bottom of the portal door.

David felt a shooting pain in the top of his shoulder. He touched his fingers to it, winced. When he looked, his fingers were bloody. And here he'd thought that arrow had missed.

Xander said, "I was thinking. What if Dad *hadn't* saved me last night?"

"Yeah?"

"Let's say I died or for whatever reason I didn't come back." He looked down at David. "What would happen to me?"

"You're *dead?*"

"Or gone forever."

David's brow furled in thought. "I think . . . if you're dead, you're dead." He pursed his lips. "If you're gone, you're gone."

Xander pointed at him. "That's what I'm saying."

David shook his head. "I don't get it."

"What happened to the family who lived here before us?"

"The dad killed everybody and—" David had a light-bulb moment. "Ahhh . . . You're saying maybe that's *not* what happened."

"What if they went over and died or couldn't find their way back?"

"*All* of them?"

Xander shrugged. "I'm just saying. As far as anyone here would know, they disappeared." He went back to fiddling with the camcorder.

David closed his eyes. "You're making my head hurt."

"No, listen. What if we just solved the biggest mystery in Pinedale's history, and we just don't have the details?"

"Or evidence."

"I'm not saying we can clear anybody's name. Just . . . wouldn't it be cool to figure it out? To know the truth?" He held up the camera and made a disgusted face. He said, "Nothing . . . just static."

"How can that be?" David rubbed his chin where the camera had cracked it when he was on the rope bridge.

Xander pushed a few buttons. His voice came through the

tiny speaker: ". . . might not want to burp or do anything too embarrassing . . ." He fast-forwarded, turning the voices into incomprehensible chipmunk-chatter. David remembered what he'd said after that: "Like scream?" Yeah, he'd done a bit of that, hadn't he? Xander got the video rolling at normal speed again: ". . . gonna get Dad and come after you." A moment later: the rude hiss of static.

"As soon as you stepped through," Xander said. He set the camcorder on the bench and unstrapped the compass from his wrist.

David rolled over. Groaning, he pushed himself up onto his knees. "Achy," he said. "All over."

Xander nodded. "Take a shower. You'll feel better." He tugged off one of the boots.

David grabbed hold of the bench, lifted himself onto it. He put his head back against the wall. "What you said? You know, finding the truth about that family?"

Xander had the other boot off and was positioning them neatly on the bench. He said, "Solve a mystery, win a prize."

David said, "There's something else about that. If what you say really did happen to that family . . ." His stomach turned over on itself. "What's gonna stop it from happening to us?"

CHAPTER

thirty-five

As Dad had done for him, Xander waited in the bathroom for David to shower. He tried being like Dad, saying comforting things and generally trying to get his brother's mind off of nearly being eaten—by beast *and* man, to hear David tell it. His brother did seem better equipped to leave his horrifying experiences in the past than Xander had been. Now that it was history, and he was alive, David didn't mind talking about it. Then again, David hadn't seen the mutilated bodies, a dead boy who was about his own age.

Twenty minutes later, Xander was sitting on his bed in the dark, listening to David ramble on about tigers and hunters and a centipede as thick as a hotdog and four times as long. David's words became slow, and he started having a hard time finishing sentences. Then, he was asleep. Xander climbed into his own bed, exhausted. He had crashed almost three hours ago only to get up again because of David's insatiable appetite for adventure. He hoped . . . he hoped *something* about David, but he was too tired to remember what it was. He fell asleep.

He jolted awake. Sirens in his ears. A noise from his dreams was his first thought, but then David was pushed up in bed, staring frighteningly at him. Smoke alarm? No, they had not installed them in this house yet. The clock on the nightstand between the beds said 2:21.

"Toria," David said, throwing off his blankets.

Xander propelled himself out of bed, letting his sheets and covers find their own way off of his body. He leaped over the footboard and landed on his feet hard enough to rattle something on the dresser.

Toria screamed. It was long and piercing, broken only by her need to fill her lungs. Then, more screaming.

Xander bounded into the hall. A dark figure bolted at him from the other end. It raced by a night-light, and he saw it was Dad, with Mom right behind. Xander arrived at

Toria's room first and rushed in. By the glow of her own night-light—*Shrek's* Princess Fiona in full ogre mode—he saw she was sitting up in bed, eyelids clamped tight, screaming for all she was worth. He skidded to a stop beside her bed. He wanted to grab her but was afraid to. He gripped her leg through the blankets. Xander would have thought it impossible, but her screams became louder, more piercing.

"Toria, it's me! Xander!" It didn't seem to matter.

Only then did he think to scan the room for an intruder. He squinted into the dark corners and at the closed closet door.

The overhead light snapped on, vaporizing the shadows and exposing not a hint of a boogeyman. Dad crashed into him. He plucked Toria out of her bed. Squeezing her to him, he said, "Honey, honey, what is it?" Then soothingly: "It's okay; it's okay."

Xander wasn't sure it was, wasn't sure of anything. But it was a parent's job to say that. Hadn't Dad spoken those words to *him* only the night before? He wondered if David had been so tough earlier because Dad hadn't been there to quash a break-down. Kind of a survival thing, conscious or not.

Mom was at Dad's side, brushing Toria's hair away from her face. She kept saying, "Sweetheart, what is it?" David stood in the doorway, his mouth a perfect *O* in the whiteness of his face.

"A-a-a . . ." Toria tried to speak.

Xander, kneeling by the bed, reached out to stroke Toria's hair. He half-expected his touch to ignite another fit of screaming.

Instead, Toria leaned her head back into his hand, as if wanting to feel it more firmly. She stopped trying to speak and concentrated on catching her breath. Three sharp little inhales, a single long breath out. At last, she raised a finger in David's direction, said, "A m-m-man . . . there was . . . there was a man in my d-d-doorway."

David stiffened, glanced over his shoulder, then hurried into the room.

Mom said, "A man, honey? What do you mean?"

Xander caught David staring at him. His eyes were wide with fear.

"I heard a n-n-oise and woke up," Toria said. "There was a man standing in my room, at the door."

"What did he look like?" Dad asked.

"Big. He filled it up, the doorway."

"What did he look like," Dad repeated. "Did you see his face?"

Toria concentrated. She made a sour expression.

"It was *dark*," she said apologetically.

"That's okay," Dad said.

"I think . . . he was hairy. He had rags for pants." She started to weep quietly.

Mom said, "Ed, call the police."

"And say what, G? They'll say she had a nightmare. Maybe she did."

Mom looked unsure.

"Daddy," Toria said.

He squeezed Toria tighter. He said, "It's okay, sweetheart. We can talk about it later."

She pushed back from him to see his face. "The man said something, Daddy."

Xander felt the skin on his forearms and the back of his neck pull taught and tingle.

Mom said, "What did he say?"

Toria shook her head. "I didn't understand it. It was rumbly, like thunder." It frightened Xander simply to hear about it. He might have screamed too. Xander gave her hair a final stroke, then moved around their parents. He tapped David as he walked by. His brother followed him out of the room.

In the hall, Xander whispered, "The big figure we saw!"

David said, "You think it was the same person?"

"It'd better be. Do you want a bunch of those things roaming around?"

"Where did he come from? We checked the whole—"

Xander stopped him with a hand on his shoulder. "I think I know. Sort of. The *rooms*."

David looked startled. "He's coming *from* one of those . . . those . . . *other worlds*?"

"Where else? That has to be it."

The implications of that swirled in David's head. Xander could see it in his eyes.

David said, "Can anything from those worlds *come through*?"

"Are you thinking about the tigers?"

David's bottom lip trembled.

Xander said, "I don't know. So far, it seems to be that big guy we saw, the one who scared Toria tonight."

David nodded. "The footprints."

They both turned their attention down the hall to the base of Toria's doorway. The floors were too clean now to pick up traces of the big man's passing.

"What does he want?" David whispered.

Xander had no answer for him.

"What if *we* stirred him up?" David said.

"You mean . . . by going through?" Xander shook his head. "Mom found the footprints in the dining room *before* we found the doors upstairs."

"But think about it. He never spoke before. He didn't *want* to be seen." David squeezed his eyes tight. "I never should have gone through. I just thought—"

"Gone where?" Dad said, coming up behind them.

The boys jumped. Dad's face grew stern, his eyes flicked between his son's faces. "Did you visit those rooms again?"

Xander bowed his head.

David said, "Yes, sir. I just wanted—"

His dad interrupted. "I thought I made it clear. Stay away from them." He shook his head. "I should have locked it up." His eyes found the bandage on David's shoulder. "That happen tonight?"

David nodded. "It was an arrow. I went—"

"Tell me tomorrow." Dad closed his eyes, then opened them slowly. He seemed tired and worried.

Probably a little more than disappointed in his boys, Xander thought. He said, "How's Toria?"

"She'll be okay. I'm gonna sleep in her room. She *could* sleep with us, but if we decide to stay in this house—"

"*If?*" David asked, sounding a little panicked.

Dad glared at him. "David, this is serious. But if we decide to stay—and that's a big *if*—I don't want her afraid of her own room. I almost have her convinced it was a dream."

They all knew better. Silence fell over them. Then Xander said, "Dad, let me do it, stay in Toria's room."

Dad shook his head. "No, I . . ."

"Then you can stay with Mom. I want to, really." He shrugged. "Least I can do."

"What about me?" David asked.

Xander said, "You can help with something else."

"I mean, I don't want to be alone. In our room. In the dark."

Xander gave him a little push. "What happened to Mr. Tough Guy?"

"He's going to sleep in Toria's room too," David said. "Double protection."

Xander said, "For you or her?"

"Ha ha."

Dad said, "Xander, are you sure?"

241

"I can do it."

"Me too," said David.

"Okay," Dad said. "Just till we figure out what we're gonna do." He nodded over their shoulders, toward their bedroom. "Go get your stuff. I'll tell the girls what's going on." He turned around, then back to his boys and raised his eyebrows at them. "And remember, those rooms upstairs are off-limits."

They nodded like twin bobbleheads.

thirty-six

SUNDAY, 2:57 A.M.

David had talked Toria into letting him sleep with her in her bed. Xander knew it had nothing to do with providing better protection for her, as David had said. He just hated sleeping on the floor.

Xander didn't mind it. He had his pillow and his blankets. The area rug beside Toria's bed took the edge off the wood floor's hardness and chilliness. He lay there now, considering the pattern of shadows the trees in the moonlight cast on Toria's ceiling. So different from the ones in his and David's room. For one thing, they were much less distinct, washed out by Toria's night-light.

Again, he thought about *The Shining*, how the house had made Jack Nicholson go crazy. What if it could happen to a whole family? What if none of this was real and they were all going crazy? Seeing things, hearing things, *experiencing* things. With Toria seeing the man—*claiming* to see the man—it was like each member of the family was slowly getting pulled in.

Xander didn't like this train of thought. It was his exhaustion talking. He made his mind think of something else.

David and Toria had fallen asleep quickly. The rhythm of their breathing was not quite in sync with each other. Toria's was a little faster and a lot quieter. Together, they sounded like distant waves breaking against a beach. Xander listened, thinking of that beach. His eyelids grew heavy. He rolled over to his left side. He adjusted his shoulder, trying to find a comfortable position. Across the room, illuminated by the Princess Fiona light, Wuzzy stared at him.

Stupid bear.

His eyes closed and he was back on the beach. He could almost feel wet sand squishing between his toes.

In the next second, he pushed himself up, fully awake. The alarm in his head had been so loud he was surprised it hadn't woken David and Toria. But there they were, shoulder to shoulder, the blankets over their chests rising and falling, almost in unison.

Wuzzy, he thought.

He stepped quietly to the bear and picked it up. Then, to the open doorway. He leaned through and peered down the hall.

Dad was there, at the junction of the two hallways. Sitting on boxes, leaning back against the wall. He was fewer than fifteen feet from the master bedroom door. Mom was probably asleep inside. Twenty feet down the other hall was the false wall, beyond which the big man presumably dwelt. Dad clutched an aluminum bat in both hands. The business end rested against his shoulder. He spotted Xander and nodded.

"Bathroom," Xander whispered. He wasn't sure Dad heard him way down there, but his father nodded as though he had. Holding the bear, Xander walked to the bathroom, turned on the light, shut and locked the door.

At the small of Wuzzy's back was a panel of controls at the small of his back. The On/Off switch was in the On position. Xander had suspected it would be, since it seemed to capture everything the family said. Toria would play back the funniest, most embarrassing, or most irritating sound bites. The bear stored half a dozen snippets at a time. Each could be up to several minutes long, Xander thought. He did know it was sound-activated and would fill its memory chips in sequence: first, memory chip number one, then two, and so on. After number six, it returned to memory chip number one. It would replace what was on that chip with a new sound. A pressure-sensitive switch in Wuzzy's right paw caused it to play back the most recent recordings. That's how Toria had driven him crazy on the trip from Pasadena to Pinedale. Now, Xander changed Wuzzy's setting from Record to Playback.

Xander squeezed Wuzzy's paw. The bear whispered, "Bathroom," in Xander's voice. Dad may not have heard, but Wuzzy had. Xander hoped he hadn't recorded over what he was looking for. He gave the paw two quick squeezes—the first returned the playback head to the beginning of the current memory chip ("bathroom"); the second brought it to the previous memory chip.

His own voice again: "Good night, guys." It was louder than he had expected. He scrambled to turn on the water. It helped mask the rest of the recording:

David answering, "Night."

Toria sweetly saying, "Good night, Xander. Thanks for watching over me."

David again: "I am too."

Toria: "Thank you, David."

Xander heard the rustle of bedding, the squeak of a spring in Toria's mattress, a bang—and he remembered bringing his head down against the night table as he settled in. Hearing it made his head hurt again, and he felt the bump on the back of his head.

Two more quick squeezes of Wuzzy's paw: Xander, David, and Toria talking.

Two more: Mom and Dad saying good-night.

Again: Dad explaining that Xander and David would sleep in Toria's room.

Xander was becoming concerned that Wuzzy had already erased the recording he was most interested in. Or . . . he remembered what had happened when David took the camcorder over: nothing but static. He hoped for something better now.

Again: His sister screaming. Pounding footsteps. Xander saying, "Toria, it's me! Xander!"

Again: Toria saying, "Who is it?" Sounding sleepy. He scrunched his brow in concentration. He held Wuzzy close to his ear. There was a creaking sound—the bedspring—followed by another. Xander thought it was a floorboard. Toria started to call again: "Who—"

A deep, rumbling voice said: "*Sas ehei na erthete na paiksei.*"

Xander's stomach tightened into a knot. Toria started screaming. Xander quickly flipped the Off button.

Xander set the bear on the counter and took a step away from it. Wuzzy appeared as sweet and innocent as a little girl in a Sunday dress, but the deep-throated voice it had recorded and shared was sinister. He did not know how he knew it, he just knew.

Toria had not been dreaming. The family was not going crazy. Their problem was different. It was much, much worse.

thirty-seven

SUNDAY, 3:25 A.M.

Now that Xander knew Wuzzy had recorded Toria's encounter with the man, Dad had to hear it. Before, when he didn't know if the bear had captured any important sounds at all, he didn't want to get Dad's hopes up or give him another reason to suspect his son was paranoid.

Xander approached him, bear in hand.

"What is it, Son?" Dad whispered. He shifted on the

box. The bat gleamed in the hallway lights. It made Xander feel better, how solid it appeared, how firmly his father gripped it.

Xander said, "We're not going crazy."

His dad offered a thin smile. "I know."

"I mean, I had kind of thought, you know . . . with the last family disappearing . . ."

"Mass hysteria?" his father asked. "You thought we were all going crazy together?"

Xander felt his face flush. It sounded ridiculous coming out of his father. "Well, I was starting to think the house was like . . . I don't know . . . like, driving us crazy, I guess." He shook his head. "Stupid, I know."

Dad slipped off the box. He touched Xander on the arm. "Not stupid. Say the house really is able to do all these weird things—drop intruders in our midst, even send you back to fight a gladiator. If it could do all that, then simply driving a whole family crazy doesn't seem like such a big deal, does it? What's more impossible: a house that makes you *think* crazy things, or a house that really *does* crazy things?

Xander nodded. "Either way, it's way off the charts, right?"

One of Dad's eyebrows curved up. "Way off," he agreed. "What's with the bear?"

Xander gave Wuzzy a little shake. He said, "Evidence we're not crazy." He turned it on and squeezed the paw. Toria's voice came through. "Who is it?" *Creak. Creeeak.* "Who—?" Then the booming voice: "*Sas ehei na erthete na paiksei.*"

As soon as the last syllable came out of Wuzzy, something overhead banged. Maybe a slamming door. Or a body hitting the floor up there. The ceiling joists creaked. Footsteps.

Wuzzy screamed in Toria's voice.

Xander turned it off. His heart pounded like a lowrider's bass speaker: *Ba-boomp! Ba-boomp! Ba-boomp! Ba-boomp!* He stared at the ceiling. No more sounds. He lowered his eyes to his Dad's face. There was fear there. *Fear.* When your dad was frightened, there was something to be frightened about.

"What was—" Xander started.

"Shhh." Dad held up one hand. With the other, he kept his grip on the bat. His eyes roamed the ceiling, but he wasn't *looking.* He was *listening.* He cocked his head, held still.

No other sounds came from up there.

Dad brought his head down to stare at the false wall. It appeared to be completely shut. Xander could not tell where it ended and the real wall began. Dad had piled boxes in front of it chest-high. Still, Xander would not have bet on their ability to keep something from coming through.

Dad watched the wall for a long time.

"Dad?" Xander whispered finally.

Slowly, Dad turned his gaze away. He snapped his head back like a pitcher trying to catch a steal, before settling his eyes on Xander. He wasn't smiling.

Xander said, "What was that?"

Dad shook his head. He said, "That was the last straw. We're out of here in the morning."

Xander felt a mixture of relief and regret. Of course, he didn't want anything to happen to his family. But he knew he would never experience anything like this again.

Dad turned and picked up a box. "Now, give me a hand." He carried the box to the false wall and added it to the others.

Xander found a safe place for Wuzzy, then started hefting boxes.

CHAPTER

thirty-eight

SUNDAY, 4:38 A.M.

Xander was back on the floor next to Toria's bed. The night's excitement had kept him going, but now his mind and body ached for a week of sleep. His eyes felt like they were made out of hot steel, his muscles nothing more than Silly Putty. He rolled onto his stomach and eased his cheek into the relaxing softness of his pillow. His head was full of images that would love nothing better than to keep him awake or give him nightmares:

his gladiatorial fight, the big man roaming their house, even all the things he'd left in Pasadena. He forced himself to once again hear the surf in his brother's and sister's breathing. He was on that beach, kicking at the water, smelling the salt, feeling the breeze . . . when the screaming started again.

He grabbed the edge of the mattress and pulled himself up. Groggy, not yet with full vision, he reached for Toria. He said, "What is it?" He felt Toria rise into a sitting position. He made out her face in the glow of the night-light—more puzzled than scared.

Beside her, David moaned, rolled over. He propped himself up on his elbows. "What's going on?" he said.

It hit Xander an instant before Toria said it.

"Mom!"

He spun and rose. He cracked his shoulder on the door frame, then crashed into the hallway wall opposite Toria's bedroom. He sprinted toward his parents' bedroom, trying to make sense of what he saw. Dad's aluminum bat lay on the floor. Boxes were scattered everywhere. His parents' door was open. No, not open—ripped from its hinges, on the hallway floor.

Xander crashed over a box. He fell on the unhinged door, got up, and grabbed the door frame of his parents' room. Only then did he realize the screaming was not coming from the room. Rather, around the corner. He spun, catching a glimpse of David beating it toward him. Xander paused long enough to hold up his hand. "No, David, stay here."

Toria came out of her room and ran toward her brothers.

Xander yelled, "David, stay with Toria. I mean it." He turned and scooped up the bat. He rounded the corner. The wall was wide open. Heavy footsteps climbed the stairs beyond, nearly lost under the sound of his mother's screams. So intent was Xander on reaching her, he nearly tripped over a pair of legs sticking out of the guest bedroom. He jumped over them, slid to a stop, crawled back. The bat clacked against the wood floor.

It was Dad. On his back. Not moving. Xander released the bat. He moved up his father's body, hand over hand. His palm pressed against his father's chest, his eyes reached his father's face, scanning for signs of life. He felt it: a heartbeat under his hand.

"Dad?" he whispered. He pushed his other hand under his father's head to lift it. It was warm and wet and sticky. He pulled his hand back, covered in blood.

"Dad!"

His father groaned. Xander heard fast footsteps.

David grabbed the door frame and almost swung through. He stopped himself, yelled, "Dad!"

Xander said, "He's alive. Mom—"

But David was already gone. He jumped over Dad's legs and pattered away, bare feet slapping on the floor.

"David, wait." Xander clutched the bat. He rose, turning away from his father. At the opening in the wall, he looked back, and braked hard. Toria had just come around the corner. He pointed at Dad and told her, "Take care of him. Stay here!" He went through the next threshold and started up the stairs.

David was at the top, hitting the landing. He turned and pushed up the switch that powered the corridor's lights.

"Mom!" he yelled and darted into the corridor.

"David, wait!" Xander yelled, almost at the top. He turned into the corridor in time to see the big man rotating around to face David, who was running all-out toward him.

Judging by his proportions in the hall, the man was not merely big, he was *massive*. He was almost naked, wearing only a tattered pelt like a diaper. He was simultaneously fat and muscular—Arnold Schwarzenegger going to pot. Broad shoulders, barrel chest, Buddha's belly. It was a body hewn and honed by strenuous and long-lasting labor, but insufficiently nourished by whatever the man could find. His flesh was covered in scars that both furrowed the skin and left ridges of discolored tissue. Dark smudges of dirt obscured even more flesh. And everywhere, sweat glistened. A long beard, seemingly made of rusty wire, burst from his face, hiding his mouth. From the tops of his sideburns, his head was bald as a rock. Fierce, dark eyes looked out from holes under a thick and bony brow.

Their mother was bent over his left shoulder. Her feet kicked in front; Xander could see her arms flailing behind the man.

As David plunged unheedingly toward the man, Xander bellowed, "No—!"

The man's cantaloupe-size fist shot forward. It hit David's head with a *crack!* David's momentum propelled his legs forward as his head flew back. His arms flung out and he went straight down. He landed on the carpeted runner with a sickening thud.

"David!" Xander yelled, almost to him. "Mom! Mom!"

Her screaming stopped long enough to yell Xander's name. Her feet kicked and kicked. Her hand kept rising and falling against the man's shoulder and back. Her efforts appeared to make no difference.

The man watched Xander approach. His face was impassive. Xander's eyes dropped to his brother, lying unmoving.

Be alive, be alive, was all he could think.

He was mentally dusting off the steps required to administer CPR—compliments of the American Red Cross and Mom's insistence that her children know the process. Could he revive David before the man stepped in to finish him off or before he carried their mother away? Didn't matter. Xander had seen the battering ram that had clobbered his brother, and he would not leave him to die on the floor.

His heart danced when David's arm rose shakily off the carpet. It reached up like a drowning man's grasp for the surface, then bent at the elbow. David's fingers found his face. He groaned.

Xander hurtled past his brother. He came down four feet from the brute. Without hesitation, he hiked the bat over his shoulder, stepped in, and swung it into the side of the man's head.

The head snapped sideways, catching Mom's hip. She began

screaming again. A bright red mark sprang up like a racing stripe across the man's temple and ear. He showed Xander his teeth. Not pretty. The man's leg-sized arm shot forward. His hand grasped for Xander's head. Xander stepped back and brought the bat down on the man's hand. The man hissed and pulled his fist to his chest. His eyes widened and seemed to sparkle with fury.

If looks could kill, Xander thought, *we'd both be dead.*

"Let her go!" Xander screamed. He stepped in, feinted another swing, then reversed out of reach. "I said, let her go! Now!" When the man didn't move, Xander swung the bat into his side.

The man grunted and heaved forward.

Xander made a grab for Mom's leg.

The brute was faster than he looked. He seized Xander by the neck with his injured hand. His fingers were like cables, cinching Xander's throat. Xander gagged, dropped the bat. The man seemed unable to squeeze harder, though his straining face reflected his desire to do so. Xander believed his neck would have already been crushed like a straw had it not been for the strike to the man's hand he had gotten in.

The man, appearing frustrated now, tossed Xander aside. Xander's head hit one of the wall lights. He crumbled to the floor. The heavy lamp lost its grip on the wall and fell on Xander's head. Everything faded. The hallway shrank in Xander's vision. Ahh . . . he was finally going to get the rest he needed. *And why not?* he thought. He knew there was a reason, but it kept slipping away.

His mother screamed.

The room swam back.

Xander remembered.

His eyes focused on the man lumbering away with Mom over his shoulder. She was looking back at Xander, her eyes so full of fear. She was pounding and scratching at the man's back, weakly now. She was giving up.

"Mom," Xander called. He tried to rise. The world spun around his head. He plopped down again. He ran his fingers over his forehead, through his hair. The same sticky warmth he had felt on the back of Dad's head. His hand came back coated in red, some of the blood his, some his father's. He was so *tired.* He just wanted to . . . he leaned back on his elbow. If he could just close his eyes for a second . . . just a second . . . then he would have the strength to get up and rescue his mother.

His mother! Had to get up now.

"Xander!"

He forced an eyelid up. David was crawling toward him. A big black-blue-yellow bruise almost radiated from his face. His left eye was not quite open, the skin around it swollen and dark blue. Blood drizzled out of his left nostril.

Xander blinked, coming back to the world. He ground his teeth together. Somebody had pounded on his little brother.

What was that joke? Nobody beats up my brother except me.

"Dae," he said.

"Xander, he's got Mom! He's got Mom!" Tears rolled over David's cheeks.

"Mom," Xander said. It felt like he was just waking up. He rolled over, got on his knees, stood. He could feel his pulse in his head, each beat feeling like a fist pounding on the inside of his skull.

Okay, he thought. *Use the pain.*

He remembered Arnold Schwarzenegger in *Collateral Damage* and Sigourney Weaver in *Aliens*—battered senseless and using their beatings to get *mad*, to get *focused*.

He stooped and picked up the bat.

The man was near the end of the hall. Only two or three doors left. He would enter one of them.

Mom's head had slumped. Xander could not see her face. He bolted for them. Each step tightened a vise around his skull. His brain throbbed.

Self-pity later. Right now: Mom.

Hoping to draw strength from it, hoping to distract the brute, Xander let go with his own piercing, animal-caught-in-a-trap scream.

Mom looked up. She appeared as stunned by Xander's primal outcry as he hoped the man would be.

The man spun around. Xander was on him again. He

ducked low and cracked the bat into a knee. The man grabbed at him, and he pulled his head back—too slowly. The brute seized a fistful of Xander's hair. The man pulled him closer. Xander lifted his foot and planted it in the man's stomach. He kicked off. Hair ripping out of his scalp. He landed on his back. The man reached for his ankle, clumps of long, brown hair falling from his fingers. Xander pushed back, pushed back. Beyond the man's reach, he rose again. Gripping the bat in both hands, he cocked it behind his head.

"You're going down," he said between clenched teeth. He was trying to psych himself up as much as anything.

He stepped in, aimed for the man's clavicle, and swung the bat over his head. It cracked against the ceiling, bringing down a plume of plaster dust. Xander felt the vibration of the sudden stop in his arms. He stumbled forward. The bat found an overhead light fixture and shattered it. Glass cascaded over Xander's head and into the man's face.

The enemy blinked against the falling glass.

Xander stepped closer. From its starting point touching the ceiling, he swung the bat backward, bringing it around like a clock's hour hand. At the six o'clock position, the tip of it pendulumed across the fuzz of the carpet, gaining speed. He brought it up between the man's legs. The jarring strike reverberated up the bat into Xander's hands and arms. The man buckled at the waist. His head came down, almost cracking into Xander's. Xander backed away; the man stumbled forward.

His hand shot up and shoved Xander in the chest. Xander flew backward. The man grabbed the bat and shook it. Xander lost his grip. He crashed into something that gave way behind him—gave way and cried out in pain. He landed on top of David, who had come up behind him to help. Xander put his hand down into David's stomach and pushed off. The boy *oophed*.

"You 'kay?" Xander yelled.

He did not wait for an answer.

"Go!" David wheezed, breathless. "Get Mom, Xander! Get Mom."

The man had recovered. He must have felt the goal was too near for these children to keep him from it. Instead of attacking while both boys were down, he had continued his trek down the hall. As Xander regained his feet, the man selected a door—second from the last. He bowed his head to clear the threshold. He stepped through.

Mom grabbed the door frame on both sides. Her straining hands made her knuckles, tendons, and veins push out against the skin.

"Mom!" Xander yelled. He reached the door. He punched his fist into the man's spine. He could have been striking a brick wall for all the good it did. He reached up to seize his mother under her arms. For just a moment, mother and son were face-to-face, inches apart. Staring into Mom's eyes, he was staring into his own—blue and wide open with terror.

He felt her breath on his face. A tear dropped from her eye and struck his cheek.

She whispered, "I love you. I love all of you."

It was the proclamation of someone who thought she would see them no more.

"No," Xander said back at her. "No," he growled. He closed his eyes and pulled on her.

His efforts and his mother's grip on the door frame kept the man from progressing farther into the room. The man kicked back. A hammer-blow to Xander's thigh. Xander yelled but would not let go. Another kick and he had no choice. Pain crumpled him. He fell to his knees, losing his grip. Mom's hands slipped off the door frame. She moved away from Xander, as the man crossed to the second door.

Xander sprung up, reaching for her. She stretched her hands toward him. Xander's bruised thigh crippled his effort. He fell without touching her. The portal door clicked open. Daylight filled the room. A frigid breeze carried in swooping coils of snow.

Xander grabbed the man's right ankle. The brute kicked back at him. Xander ducked his head against the assault. The heel, as solid as a statue's, beat against him. Once. Twice. Three times. Xander's grip loosened.

"No," he groaned. "No."

The man snapped his leg out of Xander's hands. He stepped away and out the door.

"Mooooom!" He raised his face to see her. She was smiling back at him. *Smiling.* Saying it'll be okay.

But it won't, he thought. *It won't.*

More snow blew in. The door swung past his head. He caught it in both hands. For a moment, he held it there. Then it continued its arc toward the threshold, pulling Xander across the floor on his stomach. He pulled himself forward. He got one leg in front of him. The bottom of his foot came up against the wall next to the door frame. His other leg was bent and canted back painfully. He had no time or leverage to change its position. He clasped onto the edge of the door and strained back. The door kept closing. Stuck in that aching inclination, weakened by the struggle to save his mother, he knew he could not hold on much longer.

This was a battle lost.

The door closed farther. His knee buckled. It slammed up against the wall, twisting his ankle, lifting him off the floor. He had to let go or risk losing his fingers and possibly breaking the bones in his legs.

Something bumped up behind him. David leaned over his shoulder. He stuck the bat between the frame and the edge of the door, above the door handle. Xander let go. The door cracked into the aluminum Louisville Slugger. Pinched by the door, the tortured metal screeched as if in agony. The bat pivoted forcefully to point almost straight back at the first door. It struck David's arm and spun him around. He fell on the floor next to Xander. As they watched, the door closed on the bat. When the door was one inch from closing, it stopped. The bat quivered, then the door banged shut. The severed bat fell to the floor with a ringing clang.

Xander immediately rose and clasped the handle. His arms strained to turn it. It would not budge.

The snow whipped around his legs. To the sound of a sharply inhaled breath, it disappeared through the gap under the door.

One last time, he found the strength to yell for his mother— not just his mother: his friend, a woman he adored, not only because she gave him life, but because he knew what she was all about. Anyone who knew her so well would have felt the same. She was a good person to know.

David pushed his body into Xander's side. He hugged him. He started to cry.

They both did.

CHAPTER

thirty-nine

For Xander, the tears did not last long. In their place came resolve. He gently pushed David away. The items hanging on the hooks gave him an idea of where they went. A fur-lined parka. Goggles. Gloves. On the bench was a pair of snowshoes. Someplace cold . . . wintry.

He snatched down the parka. He pulled it on. It was heavy and frumpy, floating like a cloud around his body. He tried the door, still locked. He didn't know how many items were required to unlock the door; only that you did not need all of them. He plucked the goggles from the hook and slipped them onto his head. The door was still locked.

"What are you doing?" David asked.

Xander threw him a glance.

David knew perfectly well what he was doing. What David meant to ask was: have you *thought* about what you're doing? So that was the question Xander answered. He said, "If I can get through quick enough, I can get her. I can bring her back."

"But that guy was *unstoppable.*"

"I'll think of something," Xander said, "once I'm there." He reached for the gloves. Holding them, he tried the door again. It opened easily and he looked through. Blinding whiteness everywhere. Snow swirled in. A blast of freezing air. Wind—or *something*—howled in the distance. He told David, "Come find me in twenty minutes."

David grabbed his arm. His tears were wet on his lids, his cheeks. "I want Mom back too. But, Xander, you can't—"

Xander jerked his arm away from David's grasp. "Don't try to stop me," he said.

"But you don't know—"

A muffled scream. Undoubtedly Mom's.

The brothers looked through the threshold to the unknown world beyond, then at each other. The scream had not come from there.

In the hallway, a door rattled and clicked open. Mom's scream was loud, clear, and horrified.

Xander and David bolted across the room. The door behind them slammed shut. They pushed each other through the first doorway into the hall. They looked at the last door, then down the hall toward the staircase. Halfway there, a door was open enough to see their mother's face. Her fingers were clutching, clutching, the edge. Xander yelled for her, ran. She screamed again. Her fingers disappeared. The door slammed. When Xander burst through, the second door slammed. There was water on the floor, mist in the air. The smell of the sea. He ran to the door, almost slipped. The handle was locked.

David hit the door frame behind him. "The ocean," he said.

The mist vanished into the gap under the door. The water on the floor turned into rivulets and shot into the gap, leaving not even the slightest moisture where it had been.

Xander's head pounded. Each pulse brought a new wave of pain and nausea. His eyes stung as though someone had rubbed pepper into them. He was frustrated, sad, and angry. He cast a grim expression at David. He threw the gloves onto the floor and yanked the goggles off his head. He ripped off the parka. He stepped to the bench and surveyed the items as a hunter might consider the perfect weapon.

"Don't do this!" David yelled. He was stepping up beside him.

Xander did not respond. There was a long, curved sword with a big hand guard and a rusty scabbard that might have once been covered in leather. It reminded Xander of a pirate's sword. *I definitely want that.* He pulled it down, saw that a thin, long strap ran through an eyelet in the scabbard. He looped it over his head so it hung off his shoulder. There was a three-cornered Jack Sparrow hat. Beside it, a simple scarf for tying around your head. He thought this would be less encumbering than the hat. He snapped it off of its hook.

David grabbed his arm. "You can't go like this! We don't even know if she's still in the world past that door." When Xander said nothing, David shoved him hard.

Xander sidestepped to keep from falling, and his hip hit the frame of the portal door. He lost his grip on the knot he was trying to make in the scarf. It slipped off his head. He made a grab at it, missed, and watched it settle on the floor.

He snapped his attention to David. The muscles in Xander's face were tight, his body trembled with emotion and the need to *do something.* His vision blurred, turning David into indistinct colors. He blinked, sending tears streaming down his face. David came back into focus.

The boy continued his tirade. "You can't do this!"

"*Someone* has to!" he yelled, as if it were David who had caused all of this. He knew it wasn't. The most blame lay on *his* shoulders. He shouldn't have let David go through earlier that evening, should have told Dad about David's intentions so they both could have prevented it. He shouldn't have let Dad keep watch alone; he should have done a better job helping him block the stairwell and hidden wall. He shouldn't have gone to sleep, not with all that had already happened. He shouldn't have let the man take Mom; he should have held on to her, to the death, if necessary.

All the things he had failed to do . . . all the things he had done wrong . . . They washed over him like scalding acid.

"Not like this!" David yelled back into Xander's face. "You're beat up! You're tired! You're ready to fall over!" David's head drooped. Everything about him seemed to sag, to lose its vitality. Softly, he said, "If you go over like that, you won't come back. I know you won't." His voice cracked on the second *won't*. He shook his head, knuckled away some tears. He plopped onto the bench, bowed his head. "You don't even have any clothes on. Just your boxers. How stupid is that?"

Xander's trembling subsided. He could not be mad at David for telling the truth. If he went looking for their mom now, he probably *wouldn't* come back. But he was so . . . frustrated. He knew what had to be done. He just did not possess the strength— mentally, intellectually, physically—to do it. It was like seeing a loved one trapped under a burning car that would explode at any second. Everyone has heard stories of adrenaline-fueled feats of inhuman strength, but the reality is: human muscles are no match for two tons of sheet metal.

Loved ones die. Fact of life.

But his mother *wasn't* dead, and he was not helpless. He was simply not up to the task at that moment.

"David, we *have* to get her. We have to rescue her."

David looked into his face. "I know," he said. "But we have to do it smart. We can't die trying, can we? Then who'll be here to bring her back? We'll be like that last family. *Gone.*"

Xander's shoulders slumped—with them, his spirit and whatever had been keeping him going despite injury and exhaustion. He was heartsick and discouraged. It was unimaginable to him that he didn't simply fall over dead. Were his organs really slipping over one another to pool in a heap at the base of his torso, or did it just feel that way? This must be how people lost in the wilderness felt: At what point do you muster the strength to keep going, against all odds, even after using up every ounce of energy in yourself? When do you admit defeat and lie down to die?

To Xander, David represented the logical side of the equation. Not that David didn't love their mother and want her back. He did, maybe even more than Xander did, if that were possible. For some reason, however—maybe his youth or that he had not looked into his mother's eyes as she was taken away—he was able to set aside the pure gut reaction of rescuing her immediately, at all costs.

Xander looked from David to the remaining items on the hooks. They were the other side of David's coin. They would allow him to continue the pursuit, to chase until his heart exploded. He would die in some frozen wasteland; or on the deck of a pirate ship three hundred years ago; or—if these rooms allowed it, he did not know—some moon base in the distant future. Perhaps one of those deaths was already written for him.

He knew David's way—to rest and go again—gave them the best chance of finding Mom, of bringing her back, of all of them growing old *here*, not *there*.

On the other hand, he could put on the headscarf and another of these high-seas-faring items. He could open the door—the portal—and plunge through. He could find his mother or die trying. Wasn't stopping now abandoning her? *Live to fight another day* was an expression that did not take into account the loved ones who would die because you didn't continue fighting *today*.

Feeling every movement in his body—stretching muscles, bending ligaments, the pressure exerted on every bone—Xander stooped to retrieve the scarf. He pulled it over his head and began cinching a knot in the back.

"Xander," David said, sadly. He shook his head, bowed it.

Xander heard a sniff, saw a tear fall from David's hidden face to his thigh. He was wearing pajama bottoms that were not his favorite anymore. These depicted characters from *Avatar: The Last Airbender*. He had abandoned them in favor of a more mature plaid pattern when he'd turned twelve a few months ago. Xander could not believe only one day had passed since they'd lost David's favorite pjs to the gap under the door. One day from discovering the rooms to losing their mother.

Xander leaned over David and selected a brass spyglass dangling from a hook by a leather thong. He stepped back, saw another tear fall.

"I have to," he said.

David looked up. "She went into one room, but came out another. We haven't even found out how to get back to the room we started from. We don't know enough about this for you to do any good."

"I have to," Xander repeated.

"It's stupid!" David stood up and stepped in front of the portal door. "It's killing yourself for no reason."

"Get out of my way, David."

His brother tightened his lips, scrunched his brow in determination. He widened his stance for more stability. He pressed one palm to the door behind him, the other to the wall beside the door. The doorknob was directly behind him.

"Okay," Xander said, equally determined. He stepped in to toss his brother aside.

Something banged in the hallway.

David's eyes flashed wide. "Mom!" he yelled.

Before David could dart past, Xander spun and ran into the hall. His eyes scanned for an open door or evidence of one having just closed. A voice from the other direction turned his head.

Dad was stumbling, touching his fingers to one wall for balance. Behind him, a wall fixture rocked back and forth. Dad must have knocked it as he passed. On his other side, Toria moved with him. She walked sideways, so she could press one hand to his back and grip his arm with her other. He appeared dazed.

"Dad," David called. He ran for him. The boys reached their father at the same time.

Dad's eyes stared past them, down the corridor. Xander could tell he was seeing something way beyond. He said something Xander didn't catch.

"Dad, what is it?" He leaned closer.

"Not again," Dad said. "Not again."

Xander squinted at him. "What do you mean, 'not again'?"

"Not again." Dad's face reflected something falling apart. His mouth quivered, then his cheeks, his forehead. His eyes grew big and focused on Xander.

Xander saw his father's attention coming back from that far-off place he had been. Dad's eyes focused on him, then squeezed shut. He began to moan, his shoulders heaving up and down. He was sobbing. He collapsed into a sitting position on the floor.

David stepped up behind him. His fingers caressed his father's head. He pulled his hands away. He glared at the blood on them. Then he wiped this fingers on his pajama pants. Xander witnessed his brother pulling himself together, regaining composure that he had not entirely lost. David asked, "Xander, what is it? You know what Dad's talking about?"

Through his tears, his wrenching sobs, Dad said, "I didn't mean for this to happen. Not again. Not this time. Not *her!*"

Glaring at his father, Xander said, "He *knew* this would happen!

It's happened before and he knew it." He dropped to his knees before his father. "You knew, didn't you? You could have stopped her being taken. Was this your secret? Was this your *plan?*"

Toria began to cry.

"What are you saying, Xander?" David asked, voice trembling.

Xander stood. He didn't know what to say. Had too many thoughts in his head. He turned and walked slowly down the corridor. He pulled the pirate scarf away. He let it fall from his fingers. He slipped the sword and scabbard off his neck. It clattered to the floor.

From behind him, someone called out. Dad's voice stopped him, but he did not turn around. He could not. His father's first sentence validated what Xander had suspected. It felt like being shot.

"I did know," his father said. "About this house, about these rooms."

Xander turned then. He stormed toward his father. "You *knew?* So when you said I should trust you, *this* is what you meant? Trust that our mother was going to be kidnapped, that she would be taken into some time- and space-bending place where she's all but gone forever?"

"No," their father said. "I meant things would work out. I thought they would."

Xander reached his father, still sitting on the floor. His anger frightened David and Toria—he knew and he didn't care. What their father had done was awful and it demanded his fury. They had been betrayed; their mother had been betrayed. She was gone, and his father had orchestrated the whole thing. He wanted to strike out, to punch him. He felt his fists tighten, hardening to stone. He was ready to do it, to pull back and throw his fist into his father's face.

Dad said, "I thought I could protect you. I thought I could make it different. I *locked* the door!"

Xander's anger did not know what to do with this information—his father talking protection, not harm. His putting a lock on the door at the base of the stairs did not jibe with the malicious intent he had ascribed to his father.

Xander said, "What do you mean, 'this time'? Why did you bring us here?"

Dad lowered his head. He was thinking, considering his words. His faced returned with a tight smile. He turned soft eyes on Xander. Sorrow there, regret. He said, "I thought I would be able to find my mother."

Xander jabbed a pointing finger at the door where he had last seen his mother. "Find her?" he said. "She just—" He had not really heard what his father had said, but it caught up to him at that moment. He said, "*Your* mother. What are you saying?"

The pain in his father's face was obvious. This was an agony he did not want to share. Dad said, "Thirty years ago, I watched my mother get kidnapped by someone who had come out of these rooms. I came back to get her."

forty

SUNDAY, 5:48 A.M.

"I was seven at the time," Dad said. "My father brought us here."

The four of them were sitting at the dining room table. Toria and David were tending to Dad's and Xander's head wounds. David had a nasty black eye and a bruise on his cheek and forehead that approximated the shape of the big man's fist. Dad had given him Tylenol. When Toria went for the first-aid kit, David had said he felt well enough to help her.

"Grandpa Hank?" Toria asked. She dabbed at the back of Dad's head with a Bactine-soaked gauze. It came away bright red. She wrinkled her nose at it and frowned. She tossed it in a wastebasket and stepped from behind his chair to the table where the supplies were neatly arranged.

He touched his wound and grimaced. "Yeah, Grandpa Hank," he confirmed. "We came here when he got a job at the lumber mill. He had come out earlier and found the house for us." His eyes became unfocused as he remembered. He shook his head. "It was just a house. I didn't notice anything weird. Not for a long time."

"The *noises*?" Xander said, across the table from Dad. His voice was sharp as broken bones. "How sounds here aren't right? You're saying there was none of that?"

"It was a year, at least, before I noticed anything weird."

"But you did . . . *eventually*."

Dad agreed. "I—" But Xander didn't let him finish.

"So you knew!" Xander said. He hissed and pulled his head away as David parted his hair. He was after the laceration caused by the wall light that had fallen on Xander's head. "Stop!" Xander said, pushing his brother away.

"There's a lot of blood," David said.

"Let David clean it, Xander," Dad told him. "Who knows what kind of bacteria that hallway's got?"

Xander scowled at him. "Like I should listen to you."

"I'm still your father." He stared Xander down unapologetically. He was firm about his role in his family's lives.

Regardless of mistakes, Xander thought. He said, "Could have fooled me. You lied about coming here for a job . . . and then you acted like you'd never seen the house before . . . even going to the real estate office! It was all a big scam!"

"Xander!" Toria scolded. Xander would have snapped at her as well, trying to take over for Mom already. But just as quickly, Xander knew that was wrong and unfair. Toria had often been like that, a mini-Mom. If Toria fully understood what had happened the way Xander did, she wouldn't be playing Nurse Nightingale for their father. She would be too angry and, even more, too distraught over the loss of their mother. Upstairs, Dad had said, "We'll get her; we will," and Toria had believed him.

"Wait a minute," David said. "You're the little boy in that picture?"

Dad nodded.

"That was *your* lightsaber I found?"

Dad smiled, more sad than happy. "I was a *Star Wars* freak."

"My bedroom was your bedroom!" Toria said.

"Whoa," David said, thinking. "You were that family that disappeared. So the father didn't kill his wife and kids and then himself."

"Grandpa Hank couldn't put down an old dog. After Mom was taken, he tried finding her. Every chance he could, he'd go through one of the doors and come back. Each time he got more depressed and worn down. And the house wasn't content to have taken my mother. The weird sounds continued, even got worse. When the big man started showing up again, that was it. My dad said he was afraid he was gonna go insane or that your Aunt Beth and I would be kidnapped next."

Xander noticed his father had been referring to Grandpa Hank as "my dad"—the first time Xander could remember him doing that. Xander believed his dad was back there, seven years old and reliving his experiences in this house.

Dad continued, his voice more strained. "I know it was the hardest decision he ever made, but he took us away. For our sake and his sanity, we left this house and never returned. He made us promise to never come back. I was so young, and as I got older, he kept reinforcing how important it was that we stay away."

"You should have listened," Xander said. His words were as cold as the glare he cast on his father.

Dad nodded. "Deep inside, I knew that someday I would come back and look for her, my mother. If there was no finding her, then I would at least discover what had happened and make sure it never happened again. When my dad— Grandpa—died last year, I felt released from the promise I'd made him. I couldn't stop thinking about this house."

Xander practically screamed. "So you bring us into it, your family? How stupid is that? Why would you do that?"

Dad gazed at Xander for a long time. At last he said, "I *am* sorry. I thought I could control it. Keep you guys away from the rooms. Keep *them*—" He looked up at the ceiling as if seeing "them." "Keep them out of the house. As I said, when I had lived here before, it was a long time before we realized there was something weird about the house. I thought I would have time to secure everything. I thought even if you kids found the false wall, you couldn't get up the stairs. I thought finding my mother was something I could do on my own, without anyone finding out."

David squirted ointment onto the top of Xander's head. He said, "Did you know about the rooms before your mother was taken?" Xander, David, and Toria had been told their paternal grandmother, Grandpa Hank's wife, had died in a car accident many years before. They had not talked about her much.

Dad said, "We discovered them right before she was taken. When we started hearing noises at night and finding footprints on the floors—around then is when I think my father found the rooms."

"So your mother gets taken and the rest of you up and *leave?*" Xander said accusingly.

"I didn't want to, Xander. I cried and begged to stay. And, for years afterward, to come back. I hated my father for a long time. I was an adult before I fully realized why he had given up."

Xander's face was pinched. He said, "Oh, sure. Gotta get on with your life. Can't grieve forever."

"It wasn't like that. He feared for all of our lives. And for his sanity. He came very close to losing it: he'd lost his wife, and the things he experienced in those . . ."

Xander stood abruptly. His chair flipped over backward. His head and shoulder knocked into David's arms. The gauze and tape David had been holding flew out of his hands. Xander said, "Well, *we're* not leaving! Do you understand? We're not going anywhere. I don't care what excuses Grandpa had, he never should have left his wife, your mother! I'm not leaving *my* mother here!" Tears erupted from his eyes, instantly wetting his cheeks. "You can talk all you want about saving the rest of the family, about getting away from this house before it makes you go crazy . . . But we're not leaving without her. We're *not!*" He bolted toward the dining room entrance. He shoved David so hard the boy fell, plopping down hard.

Dad stood. "Xander!" he called. "That's not what I'm saying! I—"

Xander went through the front door and slammed it on his father's words.

••••••••

Xander had no idea how long he paced the woods in front of the house. Through the trees, the sky had lightened to steel gray, then caught a bit of the approaching sun's orange fire. He dropped onto the front porch steps. Behind Xander, the door opened and closed. His father sat beside him, too close.

When he put his arm across his back to drape his hand over his shoulder, Xander pulled away.

"I'm not saying we have to leave," Dad said.

"Not yet, you aren't."

"Not at all, Xander. Not until we have your mother back. I've made some mistakes, some horrible mistakes. I endangered all of you. Your mother, my wife, has suffered, *is* suffering, because of my . . . *stupidity*. I just hope——"

The way his voice broke, the wet sounds he made, made Xander look. His father was trying to be tough, resolute. His grief was getting in his way. At that moment, it was impossible to hate the man. As terrible as his actions had been, he was right; he was still Xander's father. The grief in his face was as clear as the grief in Xander's heart. His father had not wished this on them.

Dad swallowed hard. "I hope you can forgive me, and that you'll help me set this right."

"Set it right?" Xander squinted at him.

He nodded. "Help me *work* this house. Work those rooms. Figure it all out. Get her back. Xander, *get her back!*"

Despite it all, the pain, the loss, the anger, Xander found himself smiling. There was nothing okay about any of this, but Dad's words sounded so good. They were exactly what he wanted to hear. Several sentences formed in his mouth, but he bit them back. Finally, he said, "Now you're talking." He brought his hand up around his father's back and hugged him.

Dad showed him an expression of utter relief. It said, *Thank you for not making me lose my son on the same morning I lost my wife.*

Behind Xander, the door opened again. Two pairs of feet. Toria came down a step and sat next to Dad. She leaned her head into his side. David brushed against Xander, stopped halfway down the stairs. He leaned back against the railing. Xander knew it did his brother and sister good to see him and Dad friends again.

Xander smiled at David. He said, "We're going to rescue Mom."

All of the emotions Xander was feeling crossed over David's face: sadness and worry, doubt and fear, and, finally, hope and determination. David's eyes scanned the front of the house, as if seeing it differently. Then, he took in Toria and Dad before his attention settled on Xander.

David nodded. He said, "Let's do it."

NOT THE END . . .

WITH SPECIAL THANKS TO . . .

LUKE and NICHOLAS FALLENTINE, special readers who helped set the tone;

THE FICTION TEAM AT NELSON, whose vision and expertise make my stories worth telling;

JOEL GOTLER and JOSH SCHECHTER, for their encouragement and guidance;

MAE GANNON and ANTHONY LIPARULO, for keeping me grounded and encouraging me to fly;

JODI, MELANIE, MATT, ANTHONY, and ISABELLA . . . *always.*

available now

DREAMHOUSE
KINGS

Watcher
in the
Woods

Robert Liparulo

BOOK TWO OF
DREAMHOUSE KINGS

Excerpt from *Watcher in the Woods*

CHAPTER

one

At twelve years old, David King was too young to die. At least *he* thought so.

But try telling that to the people shooting at him.

He had no idea where he was. When he had stepped through the door, smoke immediately blinded him. An explosion had thrown rocks and who-knew-what into his face. It shook the floor and knocked him off his feet. Now he was on his hands and knees on a hardwood floor. Glass and splinters dug into his palms. Somewhere, all kinds of guns were firing. Bullets zinged overhead, thunking into walls—bits of flying plaster stung his cheeks.

Okay, so he wasn't sure the bullets were meant for him. The guns seemed both near and far. But in the end, if he were hit, did it matter whether the shooters meant to get him or he'd had the dumb luck to stumble into the middle of a firefight? He'd be just as dead.

The smoke cleared a bit. Sunlight poured in from a school-bus-sized hole in the ceiling. Not just the ceiling—David could see attic rafters and the jagged and burning edges of the roof. Way above was a blue sky, soft white clouds.

He was in a bedroom. A dresser lay on the floor. In front of him was a bed. He gripped the mattress and pushed himself up.

A wall exploded into a shower of plaster, rocks, and dust. He flew back. Air burst from his lungs, and he crumpled again to the floor. He gulped for breath, but nothing came. The stench of fire—burning wood and rock, something dank and putrid—swirled into his nostrils on the thick, gray smoke. The taste of cement coated his tongue. Finally, oxygen reached his lungs, and he pulled it in with loud gasps, like a swimmer saved from drowning. He coughed out the smoke and dust. He stood, finding his balance, clearing his head, wavering until he reached out to steady himself.

A hole in the floor appeared to be trying to eat the bed. It was listing like a sinking ship, the far corner up in the air, the corner nearest David canted down into the hole. Flames had found the blankets and were spreading fast.

Outside, machine-gun fire erupted.

David jumped.

He stumbled toward an outside wall. It had crumbled, forming a rough, V-shaped hole from where the ceiling used to be nearly to the floor. Stumps of metal bars jutted out of the plaster every few feet.

More gunfire, another explosion. The floor shook.

Beyond the walls of the bedroom, the rumble of an engine and a rhythmic, metallic *click-click-click-click-click* tightened his stomach. He recognized the sound from a dozen war movies: a tank. It was rolling closer, getting louder.

He reached the wall and dropped to his knees. He peered out onto the dirt and cobblestone streets of a small village. Every house and building was at least partially destroyed, ravaged by bombs and bullets. The streets were littered with chunks of wall, roof tiles, even furniture that had spilled out through the ruptured buildings.

David's eyes fell on an object in the street. His panting breath froze in his throat. He slapped his palm over his mouth, either to stifle a scream or to keep himself from throwing up. It was a body, mutilated almost beyond recognition. It lay on its back, screaming up to heaven. Male or female, adult or child, David didn't know, and it didn't matter. That it was human and *damaged* was enough to crush his heart. His eyes shot away from the sight, only to spot another body. This one was not as broken, but was no less horrible. It was a young woman. She was lying on her stomach, head turned with an expression of surprised disbelief and pointing her lifeless eyes directly at David.

He spun around and sat on the floor. He pushed his knuckles into each eye socket, squeegeeing out the wetness. He swallowed, willing his nausea to pass.

His older brother, Xander, said that he *had* puked when he first saw a dead body. That had been only two days ago—in the Colosseum. David didn't know where the portal he had stepped through had taken him. Certainly *not* to a gladiator fight in Rome.

He squinted toward the other side of the room, toward the shadowy corner where he had stepped into . . . wherever this was . . . *whenever* it was. Nothing there now. No passage home. Just a wall.

He heard rifle shots and a scream.

Click-click-click-click-click . . . the tank was still approaching.

What had he done? He thought he could be a hero, and now he was about to get shot or blown up or . . . something that amounted to the same thing. Dead.

Dad had been right. They weren't ready. They should have made a plan.

Click-click-click-click-click.

David rose into a crouch and turned toward the crumbled wall.

I'm here now, he thought. *I gotta know what I'm dealing with, right? Okay then. I can do this.*

He popped up from his hiding place to look out onto the street. Down the road to his right, the tank was coming into town over a bridge. Bullets sparked against its steel skin. Soldiers huddled behind it, keeping close as it moved forward. In turn, they would scurry out to the side, fire a rifle or machine gun, and step back quickly. Their targets were to David's left, which meant he was smack between them.

Figures.

At that moment, he'd have given anything to redo the past hour. He closed his eyes. Had it really only been an hour? An hour to go from his front porch to here?

In this house, stranger things had happened . . .

READING GROUP GUIDE

1. None of the King kids is particularly happy about leaving everyone and everything they know back in Pasadena to move to Pinedale. Have you ever had to move away from a place you loved? How did you cope?

2. Pasadena is part of a big metropolitan area. Pinedale is small and secluded. What can you do in big cities that you can't do in rural towns? How about the opposite: What can you do in rural towns that you can't do in big cities? Which do you prefer?

3. Xander loves movies—to the point that he relates a lot of what happens around him to something he's seen in the movies. Do you ever do that with movies or books or something else? Does it help you understand situations better? Why?

4. When the Kings first find the big Victorian house, Xander gets an uneasy feeling. Have you ever had a bad feeling about something that you couldn't explain? What did you do about it?

5. "Victorian" architecture became popular during and after the reign of United Kingdom's Queen Victoria from 1837 to 1901. "Cape Cod" homes were named after an area of Massachusetts where they were popular. Do have a favorite house style? Do you know what style house you live in?

6. The Kings discover footprints in their new home. They search for an intruder or a place where people could slip into their house, but they find nothing. What would you have done if you were in their situation? What else could they have done to protect themselves?

7. Xander and David discover that the upstairs linen closet is more than a closet. What would you do if you found something so strange? Would you tell your parents? Why do you think the King boys decided to keep it secret?

8. Why do you think the guards in the Roman Colosseum threw spears at Xander? Was there anything else Xander could have done to save himself?

9. After Xander's bad experience in the Colosseum and Dad's making the third-floor portals off-limits, why was David so insistent about experiencing "going over" for himself? What do you think of his actions?

10. When David goes over, he runs into three tigers and a tribe of hunters. Where do you think he was? If you could go anywhere in history, where would you go? What would you do there? Who would you like to meet?

11. Why do you think the *Dreamhouse* portals to other worlds exist in the first place? In other words, what is their purpose?

12. The portals seem to continually shift around—for example, the first antechamber may lead to an Arctic world one time, but a pirate world the next time the Kings look. Why do you think the portals change?

13. The King children find out that Dad knew a lot more about the house than he had let on. Why do you think he kept his knowledge of the house secret? Xander and David have very different reactions to their father's lying about the house and their real reason for moving to Pinedale. Would you have responded angrily, like Xander, or more calmly, like David? Why?

THE DREAMHOUSE KINGS "DREAM THE SCENE" CONTEST

Xander and David have already battled a gladiator in the Roman Colosseum and fended off tigers in a dense jungle. Now their mother has been taken *somewhere* in time, and the kids are determined to find her. Where do you think they should look? An Aztec temple at the height of the Spanish conquest? London during the German Blitz of World War II? The Civil War?

What do they find there? What clues to Mom's location? Who helps them? Who tries to stop them? Does Toria tag along? Does Dad?

HERE'S YOUR CHANCE TO LAUNCH THE KINGS INTO AN ADVENTURE OF A LIFETIME.

Author Robert Liparulo wants to know where *you* think the Kings should go and what they find when they arrive. If he chooses your idea, he'll write it into a future Dreamhouse Kings book, making it a part of their story forever. The creator of each winning idea will be acknowledged in the novel that features the adventure, and also receive a new iPod Nano.

You have four chances to win, so find out all the rules and how to enter at www.DreamhouseKings.com.

Look for *Gatekeepers*—Book Three of the Dreamhouse Kings Series

COMING JANUARY 2009